RANDOM ACTS OF OPTIMISM

ALISON WELLS

WORDSONTHESTREET

First published 2023 by
Wordsonthestreet
Six San Antonio Park, Salthill, Galway, Ireland
web: www.wordsonthestreet.com
email: publisher@wordsonthestreet.com

© Copyright Alison Wells

The moral right of the author has been asserted.
A catalogue record for this book is available from the British Library.

ISBN 978-1-907017-64-3

All characters in these stories are fictitious and any resemblance to real
persons, living or dead, is purely coincidental.

All rights reserved. No part of this publication may be reproduced or transmitted
in any form or by any means, electronic or mechanical, including photography,
recording, or any information storage or retrieval system, without permission
in writing from the publisher. The book is sold subject to the condition that it
shall not, by way of trade or otherwise, be lent, resold or otherwise circulated
without the publisher's prior consent in any form of binding or cover other
than that in which it is published and without a similar condition, including
this condition, being imposed on the subsequent purchaser.

Cover design, layout and typesetting: Wordsonthestreet

RANDOM ACTS OF OPTIMISM

ALISON WELLS

About the author

Alison Wells was born in London, raised in Kerry and lives in Bray, near Dublin with her husband and four children. A graduate of Communication Studies and Psychology, she is now an enthusiastic librarian. Alison has been awarded residencies at Cill Rialaig, Co. Kerry. Her literary short fiction has been Pushcart prize nominated and shortlisted for Hennessy New Irish Writing, Bridport, BBC Opening Lines and Bray Literary Festival. Writing has appeared in *The Stinging Fly*, *The Lonely Crowd*, *Crannóg*, UK National Flash Fiction anthologies *Jawbreakers* and *Scraps* and New Island/RTÉ Arena's *New Planet Cabaret*. *Eat!* was highly commended in the Irish Writers Centre Novel Fair 2019. In 2020 she was a finalist with *The Exhibit of Held Breaths*. Her Head Above Water blog explores creativity and resilience.

Acknowledgements

Without The Light Pollution I Can See The Stars: *Crannóg*, autumn 2020.

There's a Café in This Story: *The Lonely Crowd*, July 2017.

All That Thinking: *Literary Orphans, Special Irish Issue*, USA, April 2014.

Letter: *Crannóg 32*, March 2013.

Flashes Of Entropy And Hope: *The New Big Book of Hope*, ed Vanessa O'Loughlin, Y books, June 2012.

Meringue: *Voices of Angels*, Bridge House, Dec 2011.

Truth And Silence: *The View From Here*, July 2011.

Unwritten: *Crannóg*, autumn 2010.

Sad About The Plumber's Uncle: *Wow Anthology*, April 2010.

Bog Body: *Sunday Tribune*, August 2009.

Dedication

For my family

For everyone making small acts of optimism even in the darkest times

Contents

Random Acts of Optimism

Random Acts of Optimism – saying I do and thinking it will last

Jenny and Tom are separated. But everyone is separated now. They live in a world where hugging might kill you and is now forbidden.

Tom's living in an apartment with someone else's things. It's his mother's. She moved into it with his stepfather before they legged it to Spain. He is a burglar in his own life. Wanting things that no longer belong to him.

Tom commutes to his job in the library. The carriage is quiet, almost empty, but the world seems full of warnings.

KEEP BEHIND THE YELLOW LINE
YIELD.
EMERGENCY HANDLE PULL DOWN
BREAK GLASS

The train lurches around a cliff top curve above the bay. He's hopeful nothing bad will happen.

Half-way to work he Facetimes his five-year-old daughter, pretend hugs her through the screen.

MIND THE GAP
MIND THE GAP
MIND THE GAP

*

Random Acts of Optimism: Getting out of bed when the legs have been taken from under you

Cynthia gets up in the morning and visits the rooms of the house.

This is the circuit. Across the bedroom carpet, onto the landing, Matthew's room, stuck in time, the spare room, door forever shut. Downstairs, that place in the hallway where her chest tightens and her hands go into fists, out through the kitchen to the back door where a stray cat is waiting optimistically for her to take notice and put a little milk or something else into the bowl.

The phone rings. It startles her. It's Madeleine. They were supposed to meet for ages but now with all the restrictions they are like two astronauts in an airlock waiting for the go-ahead. Why didn't we do it while we could? Are the buses even running? I don't know – there's nothing on the roads, no planes, not even anyone on a bike?

'Why did we put it off?' Madeleine says, her voice robust and familiar. 'It's not as if we thought we had loads of time. At my age I don't even buy unripe bananas ... You have to be optimistic though, don't you? Or you'd go bananas yourself ...'

'Look at the Italians singing from their apartments.' Cynthia agrees. She remembers. 'I did see a man walking past yesterday. He was wearing a mask and seemed in a hurry. Maybe he was off to rob a bank.'

'Good luck to him, the shysters,' Madeleine remarks.

The cat is still waiting. Cynthia opens the door and feeds him. The sun is blazing away like there's nothing going wrong. While he's eating, she hears a sound. There's a robin fluttering round the pond and darting in and out of the bushes. She hopes the cat won't notice.

*

Random Acts of Optimism: Hoping a new job will make him feel something

It's eerie, arriving in this apocalyptic world. The plaza, the café, the steps, forlorn of people.

Tom had been in the library job only two weeks when the doors shut. The families were in after the school run when they got the news of lockdown. You heard about toilet rolls, but no-one spoke about the armfuls of books – gathered in panic.

When the library itself closed, they'd asked staff to volunteer on the Community Call. Those available to help, no family commitments or underlying conditions. Whatever underlying conditions he might have (perpetual fear, existential angst) it wasn't what they were referring to. As for family commitments ...

He'd felt sprung into action, focused for the first time since the separation, since moving into his mother's apartment now that she'd popped into an episode of *A Place in The Sun*. About the volunteering, she'd said on the phone from Sitges: 'You might as well keep yourself busy.'

As he nears the library headquarters, he is close to the harbour. He passes the poster puns for the fish restaurant. *No better plaice. We're not codding you. You'll never get batter.* Like musical earworms they play around his head surfacing – like flying fish! – when, later, at breaktime he replaces one sort of hallowed solitude for another, making his way to the closed café where invisible staff have placed sandwiches filled with tuna, salad or barbeque chicken in the fridges.

ONLY ONE PERSON BEHIND THE COUNTER AT A TIME
WIPE DOWN SURFACES AFTER USE
KEEP TWO METRES APART

When he told her about the breakup his mother said. 'I wouldn't want to lose touch with my granddaughter ... When your Dad and I ... Well ... women today, they've got more freedom, they could up sticks ...'

Celia-Jane is with Jenny in the family home. That's the way it is right now. What can he do about it? He stands near the large windows looking out at the outdoor tables and the green space and there is no-one there.

The library level upstairs is temporarily out of bounds. The building split into potential contamination zones, areas he can no longer go into. In the basement office, he and his colleagues speak to each other in bursts, interspersed with long periods of quiet diligence. He's nervous of the sudden ringing of the phone. Everything the callers might possibly need. Mostly they ring with shopping lists. A carton of milk, a few sausages, one of those pies in a tin. Are you sure you don't want anything else?

5 Easter eggs and some wholegrain yogurt.

Chocolate – not those tiny bars.

Bread, milk, rashers and tea.

Do you know anyone who could deliver me a few bags of compost?

Tom's not sure, there are volunteers to drive people to the doctor's but is gardening an emergency?

'I'll see what I can do.'

'You're awful good.'

Awful good ... At the end of the shift, he takes the train home to his mother's apartment.

SEATS ARE NOT FOR FEET

He gets a picture of him and Jenny, stretching out on the sofa together, toes touching, surrounded by the everyday chaos of the family home, blankets, games and mugs and Celia Janes hand drawn pictures on the fridge, all the clutter filled with a significance he now recognises as love.

*

Random Acts of Optimism: getting up again although nothing has changed

Cynthia gets up in the morning and visits the rooms of the house, taking in all the objects heavy with memory. For once, she opens the door of the spare room. On the table a stack of car magazines, a coffee cup with a pale blue layer of mould. She retreats to the landing, heads towards the stairs, swaying, slightly dizzy, holding the rail as if on the deck of a ship. She's not sure what she ate yesterday, the days running into each other, the food in the cupboards seeming to move backwards, bit by bit to reveal tuna from ten years ago, dried lentils, black-eyed peas.

John got them the handheld phone for the kitchen but the one in the hallway is old style, weighty and black. Her heart hammers as she passes that place. She doesn't like picking up the phone now.

She never liked phone calls, even before, disliked that gap between dialling and wondering was it the right number, the right person, trying to find the right words. She's alright calling Madeleine, dials without thinking, like the numbers are in her fingers. How are you over there, Madeleine? She's only three stops on the train. She might as well be in America, or Sweden like Matthew.

Madeleine tells her to ring the Community Call to get her shopping delivered. The government's organising it.

'It's like the time they sent us the tablets in case of nuclear disaster. I think they're still around somewhere.'

'They must be out of date by now ...'

'Do you think it's out there floating round in the air, the Covid?'

'That's what they seem to be saying ...' Cynthia looks through the glass.

'Do you think they'll find the paddleboarders – the girls who drifted out to sea? I'll say a prayer for them anyway. You have to hope ...'

Cynthia doesn't say anything. There were times praying didn't make any difference.

Tom answers the phone to a woman called Cynthia. He's still working on Community Call, taking down shopping lists. She seems a little confused, or the line is faint, or both.

'Just two chops, not four. The pack was too big last time. My husband died. I forgot.'

'Just one set of chops then?'

'Yes, please. And tuna that's in date.'

'Anything else?'

'What I really miss is the library.'

'I'm in here now,' Tom remarks.

'Where?'

'The library. We're operating the Community Call from here. We can send you books. What sort would you like?'

Cynthia is interested in Swedish noir. Her son Matthew moved to Sweden so she wonders what it would be like. Tom isn't sure if her first insight into Sweden should be dead bodies in icy woods. Should he send her a travel guide instead? Or is that tactless given the 2km restrictions? She keeps asking him if he's read anything good lately. What he didn't tell anyone when he got the job at the library is that he doesn't really read.

*

Random Acts of Optimism – going outside

Cynthia is on the landing. Even before the lockdown they used to stockpile toilet rolls in the attic. They're probably still there. She looks up, warily. It might as well be Mount Everest. She stands at the open door of Matthew's room surveying the long space

14

between her and the bed. She makes her way across, as if she will reach him. She sits on the bed, an uninvited stranger. She's nearly seventy. He's a forty-year-old man. When does she think he's coming back?

'When are we going to see each other?' Madeleine said last time. 'Do you do the Zoom Cynthia?'

'I do,' Cynthia said. 'Do you?'

'I'd rather shout over the side passage.'

'I'm not that good at hearing,' Cynthia protests, 'your side passage is too far off.'

She does the Zoom with Matthew, when he doesn't cancel. Maybe they should revert to the phone, so he won't have to try so hard. The Zooms are in the dark, him in his kitchen with only a couple of downlighters. She thinks of Mastermind, him in the chair, listening to her interrogations. She sees him in the dimmed light of his bedside lamp, aged three or four, sleepy-eyed under the covers listening to her reading a story. She turns instinctively to the bookshelf, *Alice in Wonderland*, he loved the arrogant Queen of Hearts, Humpty Dumpty. He'd slap his own head, with a knowing laugh. 'Nothing makes sense!'

Down the stairs, ever lengthening, like something from *Alice*, across that place in the hallway. Cynthia feels queasy, a kind of travel sickness, something pulling her backwards when she's trying to go on.

She hears post falling into the hallway. There's a flyer *To the householder*. There's a bill that still has John's name on it. She pauses, hearing the quiet of the street outside. She taps the door as if for good luck, just to let the outside know she knows it's out there. The last time she went out it was to the corner shop. She needed bread, she already had toilet rolls. There was a sense of adventure, putting on her mask and walking into the empty streets.

The young lad at the counter was reading *Crime and Punishment*. He placed it on the counter, splayed, cover up. As she paid for the bread and gravy granules, she gestured toward the book. 'I always loved the Russians ...!'

'I'm studying English Lit in Sligo,' he said. 'Well, I'm there and not there. With the pandemic, they said not to go back. At least we're not incarcerated in our residences.'

He had that soft look around the mouth and cheek, that nod to childhood, uncertainty underneath. Like Escher's stairways, going everywhere and nowhere all at once. 'I suppose *The Brothers Karamazov* is next or *The Gulag Archipelago*,' she said. As she gathered up her purchases and left the shop tears came to her eyes – nothing unusual – these days you got the feeling you had left all sorts of things behind – but he reminded her of Matthew, of the boys in her English class year after year with their big ideas and all the things that might go wrong.

Now when she opens the front door and thinks about going out, she doesn't feel adventurous anymore.

*

Random Acts of Optimism: Thinking you can make a difference

'Tom! Hello!' As if she knew him. 'I didn't get you the last time,' Cynthia says to him, 'it was a nice lady instead. But the books you sent the time before were a great distraction. I liked the one about the murder on the cruise ship. The ending, I never saw that coming!'

Tom says he's surprised how much – excuse him for saying – the older people seem to like the murder. Black books with yellow type or fog or splashes of red. Dead girls in the Dublin mountains, crime lords, body parts in suitcases. 'It's flying off the shelves. We can't keep up.'

Cynthia jokes 'Maybe there's some frustrated people stuck in the house together trying to get some tips on where to hide the body?'

She's asking him again for recommendations, assumes he's

16

up to date with reading. 'Imagine being trapped inside a library!' She tells Tom she was an English teacher and the thing about the classics is that – love, betrayal, revenge, fear, confusion – nothing much has changed. Whether it's Othello getting the wrong end of the stick or Hamlet not being able to decide what to do, it could be you or I she says. She laughs again. 'Except for the body count at the end of the play ...'

'Tom, I need something to keep me going. It's just me now on my own. I hardly hear from Matthew. Do you have children?'

'I've a daughter – she lives with her mam.'

Tom thinks she's gone, then ... Cynthia's voice coming back out of silence.

'What happened? What's the story there?'

Jenny had asked him if he'd wanted to move out and he hadn't protested. Death by fence sitting. He's not going to tell Cynthia that. 'Sometimes there doesn't seem to be any link between what you do and how things turn out, it's random ... Like nothing you do will make a difference.'

Another pause from Cynthia. 'Yes. I don't know what happened with Matthew. I think we've both decided that we don't get on. I suppose sometimes we get mesmerized by our own stories.'

He doesn't know what else to say so he tells her about a woman who returned a book two years too late. The book was called *Successful Time Management for Dummies.*

In the afternoon he is authorised to go upstairs to select the books. When Tom reaches the library level, rising up from the gloomier admin floor below, the view over the sea opens out from the wide windows. The sun like a whisky shot, hitting him right in the chest, pale skyline, weird, surreal clouds from the opening credits of *The Simpsons*. The walls of timber shelves and the books – now toppling and askew – are bathed in yellow easterly light. He walks the long length of the book stacks to the window at the children's area, looks down on the peopleless street, then makes his way through the silent library to choose books for Cynthia.

*

Random Acts of Optimism – opening a book

When Cynthia does the circuit, sees Matthew's empty bed and the long stretch of carpet from the door, she relates to Tom's words. The fact that, of all the people Matthew had bumped into at an office conference, it happened to be a woman from Sweden and he ended up living ... what? ... over a thousand miles away – instead of down the road. The fact that some particles had mutated and now a disease with the same name as a cold virus was a deadly plague. When she went past that place in the hallway and shook from head to foot – almost invisibly so if there had been anyone there, they wouldn't have noticed – she understood what Tom from the library meant. Would anything she had done have changed the way things turned out?

The book bag is by the front door. She takes out the novels that the man – Tom – sent her from the library. She flicks open the pages of one – will it be any good? Nowadays it'll be a wonder if it distracts her from the quiet or gets her back to sleep at night. It's like Madeleine's bananas, when you start off a book you've got to hope you'll still be around for the end.

This time when she goes to the backdoor, the robin is waiting. He looks pleased with himself. There's no sign of the cat. She hopes the cat is alright.

*

Random Acts of Optimism – opening your eyes and noticing the signs

Sometimes Tom thinks that someone is trying to tell him something.

On his lunchbreak walk:

18

FOOTPATH WILL END IN 40 METRES

'We've run out of road.' He'd said to Jenny. That was one way of putting it and saying made it so. He'd run out of imagination. Getting cold feet after the fact was understandable – it didn't mean it was wrong. Even if reading *Alice in Wonderland* to Celia Jane through the glass of his computer screen made no sense at all.

MIND THE GAP
MIND THE GAP
MIND THE GAP

Occasionally he drives his car on empty roadways. The signs suit him better.

KEEP YOUR GUARD UP
HOLD FIRM

'What about these books I'm getting you?' Tom asks Cynthia.

'I've gone off murder, it's keeping me awake. All those dead people lying round and it's not as if I can do anything to help.'

'Alright so, I'll see what else I can find ...'

At first the books had been just books, dead wood, lining the shelves, toppling now, in various states of disarray since the stock was depleted. But now he'd become aware of their internal noise, the volume of words, wanting to be heard. He tries to explain it to Cynthia.

'The jabber of humanity,' she replies in words that make a satisfactory landing.

Tom agrees, 'I mean yeah, all those stories, true and made up, everything that could happen.'

'I think Borges had something to say about that,' Cynthia remarks. 'What I like when I open a book is not knowing what

I'm going to find. And how when I close a book the story keeps on going in my head.'

When later he Googled Borges, it gave him a) librarians that could not find anything of meaning and were driven to despair, and b) libraries that contained all the possible books ever written or that could be written – sensible or senseless. All the choices he could have made, how things might have been different.

He'd met Jenny in a library, laughing because a book called *Chaos* had fallen off a shelf and hit her on the head. The book was about how things that seem random and improbable were part of a larger repeating and expanding pattern that could only be seen once you stood back. Everyone knew about the butterfly and the hurricane but maybe it didn't only work for bad stuff – maybe there was something that could push things back the right way so they could turn out good.

He was systematic, scanning the shelves, always checking the rapidly depleting crime area or the white, flower-decked volumes for the requested 'light reads', but the way he found books was sometimes what Cynthia would call *serendipity*. He flicked open *Diary of a Plague Year* by Daniel Defoe, *Three men in a Boat, Silence in the Age of Noise* and found words that seemed just right.

On Wednesday, someone has written down a message from Cynthia.

Tom, thank you so much for the books you sent last time. Some very thoughtful choices. I slept better.

When he has finished selecting that day's books to be delivered, Tom stands at the window looking out at the horizon. Improbable cloud formations in an ever-changing sky. A young boy waves to him from the street below. Tom waves back from the empty library, laughs out loud.

The train home is busier these days, full of people speaking: their dog went to the vet, the landlord is a bastard, she's nervous now the husband has just died and she doesn't drive, the interview is next Friday but it might be too much of a commute, he had to call the out the plumber, she has to go into the hospital next Tuesday, the last time she was waiting two hours even though the appointment said ten o'clock.

Sorry Cynthia but the jabber of humanity sometimes does his head in.

*

Random Acts of Optimism – going on with no instructions

Cynthia picks up the book that Tom sent from the library.

Sometimes you look at a word and it no longer makes sense, the letters loosen and come apart and it looks like some random juxtaposition that doesn't mean anything. The same but utterly unintelligible. Like the house each morning without John in it.

The doorbell rings, Cynthia opens it and scuttles back, blinded, words lost to her. She points inside the door and hopes the delivery man will drop the shopping and leave. Later she will put on rubber gloves and get the Jeyes fluid and wipe everything down. The man asks her if she's alright. She nods, waves him away. The space between them in the hallway is the place where it happened. When she closes the door behind him she feels her teeth gently pressing on the skin of her knuckles.

*

Random Acts of Optimism: leaving your umbrella behind

Before Tom leaves for the library, his mother rings from Sitges. She's vaguely agitated. She hints at returning. 'It isn't how I thought it would be. It's sunny every day, you never have to wonder. Back home you had to hope for the best and take your chances.'

He opens the door to rain. But it's brightening up in the distance. Who knows? It might clear up later. He brings an umbrella to the train just in case.

PLEASE GIVE UP YOUR SEAT IF AN ELDERLY OR INFIRM PERSON NEEDS IT

He imagines the older people at home, looking out the kitchen window, putting on the kettle, holding the first cup of tea or coffee of the morning, adjusting their windowsill pots of watercress, padding around in their favourite slippers, opening the door to pick up the milk from the doorstep. In the kitchen having their porridge or toast with thick cut marmalade or maybe a boiled egg and later getting dressed and later again looking at the clock and thinking *wasn't there a number for books, why don't I give them a call?*

He has not heard from Cynthia in a while. When he is fulfilling the other orders, he finds items Cynthia would like and puts them aside. So he can find books that are just right, he reads more and more, consumes other people's lives.

These are the books he finds: a family saga set among olive groves, an intrepid female explorer, a comedy set on a cruise ship, a wholesome period drama, a detective story about a lost cat and – apart from a book called *Remains of the Day* – no murder whatsoever.

Random Acts of Optimism – thinking that hurricanes might create butterflies

It's Tom on the phone. 'Tom from the library.'

'Oh!' says Cynthia, standing in the hallway. 'Oh! I haven't asked for anything.'

'I know, just wondering ... Are you alright? I didn't hear from you ... The library's open now – we can still send you books if you're cocooning.'

She leans against the wall, glad of its solidity. 'I'm not sure I'm 'cocooning" she replies, dryly.

'I've some picked out ... I'll send them anyway.'

She doesn't have much to tell him, but he seems happy to talk. He tells her a story about how, just before lockdown a man returned a book that had been eaten by his puppy. The book was called *How to Train your Dog.*

Later she wonders what Tom will send. She likes the feeling of waiting to see. She looks around the kitchen, the tea canister (hers) and coffee canister (John's), the swanky metal bread bin he bought, the glass butter dish from her mother, the key holder Matthew made in woodwork class aeons ago. All these things, sitting, so familiar, innocent, expectant, almost hopeful, anticipating that something else will happen. She hates to disappoint them. She decides to make her own bread, give the weighing scales a trip out of the cupboard. Like Madeleine's bananas, it seems an act of optimism, doing something, believing she'll feel like eating it.

On Tuesday when the books arrive, she brings them in from the porch. In the inside cover of a book, a postit note. *Maybe I'm not supposed to do this, but if you need any help, here's my number, I live nearby. Tom. PS I watched the movie of Hamlet. Quite good.*

Quite good. A man of few words, like John.

A knife-like chink of light falls across the place in the hallway where it happened, as slim as the bookmark in her hand. She cries now as if she will never stop. John had been infuriating, opinionated, self-contained. In the marriage, a thread of loneliness. There were plenty of times she might have walked away, the spare room door closed against her, his coffee and engineering magazines. But that was just one side. She remembered coming up to meet him one day at the bus stop, they'd been heading out somewhere. As she approached, he finished reading and put his book inside his jacket pocket. But it seems to her now that she'd married him because of how gently he'd put a bookmark between the pages of his hardbacked copy of *One Hundred Years of Solitude*.

A week later she walks, carrying a bag of books, across the place in the hallway where her husband's heart stopped. She goes out of the door, tapping it once, just to say things will probably be alright.

*

Random Acts of Optimism: thinking you've solved the mystery

He hears her voice first.

'It's you,' says Cynthia, 'Tom isn't it? You've been sending me book selections. We chatted on the phone. We joked about murder.'

She is taller than he imagined, more solid. He gets up from the library desk. He wants to hug her.

KEEP 2 METRES APART

She smiles, holds up a book. I'd read this one already. Remains of the Day. It looks like it could be about murder, but it wasn't – even though there was a butler.

'What's it about then?'

'Wasted chances.'

Tom has a look. He's not much of a reader but it's a slim book.

Later Tom walks around the library, seeing if anything leaps out. There are so many stories, any one of them could be right. The next time he's travelling he takes the car. His mother's apartment is by the motorway. He drives right past. When he sees the signs approaching – he keeps an open mind – they could mean anything.

PROTECT YOURSELF
PROTECT OTHERS
STAY AT HOME

There's A Café In This Story

There's a café in this story. The details of the café don't matter, so let's begin with ubiquity: a table, plastic flowers. The menu is leaning against condiments conjoined in a metal holder, the pepper straight and military, the salt askew. He thinks *square peg, round hole*. His finger is pressed against the plastic laminate of the otherwise stylish menu card as she passes the window, resplendent in a heavy wool coat. *Resplendent*, it's a word he now uses even when there isn't any proper reason for it. It's a word they joked about together once, it sounds romantic, although in truth, her coat is of the usual kind. He sees her passing by the window although he is set back from it, at the wall, among the furore of furniture, chair legs, people legs and the negative space between them. He sees her coming in the door and struggling in through the furniture and people and his heart flips like the marshmallow in his hot chocolate. It's that sort of place.

There's a café in this story but more often the man makes instant at the work tea station. He is the father of a newborn, he is the sales manager for a product that is too complicated to explain to his wife. That first time he was carrying coffee back to his desk when he looked out of the window and saw the woman going down the street. She was walking in the direction of the sea. Later he discovered that she worked in the toner shop between there and the promenade.

There's a café in this story but at home his wife is breastfeeding the baby. She is so thirsty and she cannot move. She should have remembered the glass of water the nurse recommended, she's an old hand, this child is her third. Noah, the toddler is on the floor, playing with his ark – his toy choice inevitable. Gemma is at school. The wife's breast is sore as the baby feeds, his see-through fingernails claw at her, sharp stabbings run through her. His wife is soft, malleable and melting, skin, muscle, bone and milk. She arranges pillows and the voracious child and tries to stay upright. She should be drinking that water but she aches for coffee.

*

The woman sits down in front of him and her hair smells of the sea. Some of it is still tucked in her collar and its dark russet tones compliment the tan of her coat. She takes off gloves and he notices her small hands. There are ink stains here and there, it must be from the cartridges. She laughs when she sees him sipping the hot chocolate. He likes her laugh and she likes his eyes and the way they take her in. How they understand each other.

She peers into his mug. 'Marshmallows,' she says, smiling. She should choose the same now as him, but, after the long morning in the shop, waiting, and the nights she cannot sleep she longs for coffee instead.

When he's not here with her, and when he's not on the road – motorway pit stops; airport hotel meeting rooms, or industrial estates – he spends sombrous afternoons in the office scrolling sales figures in a soft carpet silence, punctuated only by collegiate exchanges, or the triumphant staccato of a closed deal on his mobile, a brief intense high note that quickly falls. On good days he retains the feeling of his lunchtime walks, white horses coming into the bay, wide skies, the stretch of alto cirrus. Standing at the pier he reaches up, his arm held aloft, the gaps of his ribcage widening like the tines of a cloud on the move. Then his head and knees bend in a vulnerable plié, this pluck and zing of desire, those low notes of guilt. Back in the office, weary, he stretches again. It's like this: when he sees the woman passing his window on the way to the sea, it feels as if she traces each one of his beached, bleached ribs and the ache between them.

The next time they meet in a seafront café outdoors with the sounds of the boats and the clink of their anchors, the gulls in wild congregation, flapping and racing at the water. He enjoys the freedom of it, the air and the light. He looks at the side of her face, her features more definite now than that of his wife, her hand rests on the table. It's there to take. He takes it. The anchors clang like bells. He says her name, they laugh together; the sea and sky around them are infinite and possible.

At home, his wife has put the baby down for a nap to the sweet slowing notes of his musical mobile. She goes to make a coffee and then stands for a long time at the deserted kitchen island, holding her mug, staring with amnesia. By the sink is his coffee from the morning, still full, now stagnant and separating, the cup discarded in haste. His wife moves slowly to the kettle.

Sometimes he drives long, long roads, to sell to clients a product that is too complicated to explain to either his wife or the woman in the café. Miles and miles of road fall away beneath his wheels and it seems that journeys contain whole lifetimes. Now, months on, beyond a toll booth appear the trusses of a large bridge, traversing in the still dark some invisible void. Girders, arms up, recall to mind how he and his wife met, in a trendy café of steel and shiny surfaces. They were in their early twenties, summer jobs, waiting tables, they bumped into each other and rotated round, arms and trays raised, cogs in a wheel fitting together, laughing.

Driving across the bridge, segments of dawn scenery flash through the metalwork. In the café – the haunt of long-legged creative types – everything moved very fast. It was skinny lattes, ciabattas and steam whoosh, glimpses of her face through slants of shelf, elbow, tea trays. Now, in his periphery, frenetic bridge trusses give way to angled tableaus: his wife, long hair askew, holding up wallpaper against the walls of their first home, laughing as he comes close to assist. Him leaning against her back, the smell of glue. A man stretching to put the star on the tree, the small armed, hug beseeching of his children.

He remembers his wife laughing suddenly, thought-struck, sitting on the sofa with Gemma and Noah and the new baby in his arms. "That café has a lot to answer for," she said. And going back further to the beginning: the scooped out dip of his wife's hip, the coffee scent of her in bed, her heavy breasts and round shape containing an infant, her hair thick and luscious. His hand on her stomach as they fell asleep. All because of a café.

*

A café in January of both hopeful resolution and cold backdrops, the decorations torn down, his palm flat against cool Formica. The squall of the wind in the door as it opens and closes. She is wrapped up in a coat, and scarf, her face barely visible. *Resplendent* he thinks. As soon as she sits down he takes hold of her chilled fingers, his hand is coffee cup warm.

There are details that build up over time, the first, shyly uncertain pleasantries, umbrellas under the table, ankles knocking against the metal legs and then against each other. He wonders if he will remember, in the years to come, this particular café, or that, the gurgling whorl of the steam, the particular intensity of that sound rising to a crescendo, the table decorations, prints on the wall, the specific timbre of a certain café's hum. Or will the cafés all merge, with all their combined sensations of exhilaration and regret?

The coffee frother whines and at home the infant makes that long thin waking surprised cry. His wife puts the muslin over her shoulder and lays the baby against it. Like a snippet of the past, two waiting staff chat, the male makes a joke and the female takes the teacloth from her shoulder and flicks it at him. At the table, holding the woman's hand, he winces. At home his wife is so weary, her arm raised adjusting the muslin. She aches for coffee, the future and the past.

*

Long roads bring him to motorway cafés; greasy spoons where the waitress languorously polishes to the mutter of the radio and the hum of the coffee machine and the spit of the frying pan.

He sits in the border of night and morning looking out to the blazing forecourt and the ink of the night beyond. Trucks with wheels the size of a man thunder into the car park and behind him he hears the clink of a spoon in milky tea. These are the cafés where you might meet a stranger and share a story with them, tell them things that no-one else knows, things that eat at the heart of you, make you feel you've gnawed your own bones clean. The kind of café you arrive at and leave from alone. He thinks about the other cafés where the woman walks through the door and her face fills with joy to see him and he tells her things about himself that she seems to understand.

It's those kind of cafés he thinks about when he packs up his car with the little he needs. As he drives away, he begins to picture the woman in the car beside him. She would be familiar and new, leaning forward slightly with her hands pressed into the braille of the seat cover, deciphering old tales. Long black roads, take out coffee in cup holders, the woman's silhouette emerging in a dawn light that makes silver of the roadway.

By 4am he is well on his way, his wife has just finished the baby's early morning feed. She sits in the dark, sipping coffee, imagining him on the road. When she is finished she washes the coffee cup carefully. She stops, holding it for a moment, looking out the window into nothing, then stretches right up, ribs widening, to put it away.

The man keeps driving along the silver road. As it gets brighter, he sees the gauze of clouds high in the atmosphere. As it gets brighter, he pictures the woman waiting alone in the café, *resplendent*, her hand flat against the pine, Formica, oilcloth, steel, the hiss and whine of the frothy coffee maker, the cold blast of air in the door every time it opens, gulls and anchors, umbrellas, condiments askew, plastic menus with their innumerable choices. The servers rotating around her like cogs in a finely tuned clockwork, arms aloft, laughing.

The Memory Jar

In the galley kitchen with the painted white units, Sarah decanted her memories into the jars. Next, she added labels, dating them like her mother's homemade jam or her father's photo album; Summer 2010, Christmas 1989, Autumn 1977. Bending down, she set the jars in chronological order along the transparent shelves of the special fridge.

The Cat slunk into the kitchen. He was grey, with some darker black flecks. He slid around her legs purring with that intense internal motor. Sarah stared blankly at the Cat before briefly running her hand along the soft nape of his neck.

The jars looked pretty, all in a line, with their frog-spawn-like contents. Sarah ran her fingers along the lids, peering at the tadpole memories, aware only vaguely of what was inside. Instead Sarah recalled the clinic's colourful room, decorated like a nursery – with crayons and teddy bears scattered about. She's wondered if the procedure was completely effective. She remembered the scientist's friendly reassurance.

'Memories are distributed across the brain in such a way that we can't purge every trace. But we take just enough.'

What remained, the consultant explained, was like a handful of pieces from a jigsaw, little nudges to what the whole might look like but not enough to form a picture. She'd nodded, thinking of golden leaves scattered from a single tree.

The memory harvesting technique had been developed out of work on degenerative brain disorders. New quantum scanning techniques meant that particular memories could be identified and extracted. The siphoning was quite painless – like having your ears syringed. The memories were sent back in sealed plastic containers. Sarah preferred the pretty jars with their gingham lids and ribbons.

Sarah closed the fridge and went into the kitchen, tore two kinds of lettuce from the heads, sliced tiny tomatoes in half. She made salad, poured on dressing and tossed in walnuts as an afterthought. She broke eggs into the pan and scrambled them. She put it all on a plate and went to sit at the table. Steam rose from the eggs. She put her hand against the tablecloth. Everything was clean and ordered, quiet. The cat slipped around the table leg and she felt surprised.

In front of her was a printout listing details of the extracted memories. Sarah could read about her life as if it was someone else's; measles at four, that trip to the seaside in 1983 when she'd first become aware of boys, details of relationships and at the end of the document, two names: David and Catherine. These names sent scatterings of pain across her cranium. Sarah tapped her head three times with her fingers. She turned on the radio and was soothed by the mellow, oval tones of a violin concerto. The announcer revealed that the piece was performed by the classical virtuoso Naoko who had taken up a cultural residency in the city.

The next day Sarah travelled to work on the train. At the station she saw herself in the papers – a small front-page report on the memory procedure. In the carriage, she scanned faces, wondering if she should know them. The memory extraction technique was exacting but there could be collateral loss. Sarah took out her phone and flicked on the facial recognition app. The phone scanned her personal database and told her that she was surrounded by strangers. It was comforting to know.

In the office her colleagues looked at her with unexpected tenderness. Her job in the law firm mainly involved archiving completed cases. On the heady upper floors with the thin sharp lemon light, entering rooms, placing the files within their strong metal containers, the feeling was of a dream with no beginning, the slipped skin of a snake.

Those days at work, repeating and repeating: the kindness of

32

colleagues and dust motes spinning in the archive room, the clickety-clack mantra of the train coming home, dark tunnels giving way at stations to instances of life. Strange faces, another and another until one stood out. A young oriental woman, her hair cropped elfin style, looked straight at Sarah, then through her to her reflection and back. Sarah felt unsettled, but her phone reported no connection with the woman.

On Saturday morning coming into the quiet kitchen, Sarah saw the jars lined up on the window, the glass in sunlight acting as a prism, making unreachable rainbows. She couldn't remember leaving the jars there but didn't move them. At her legs the Cat meowed. Sarah felt an extraordinary rage.

That afternoon her brother Samuel came round for coffee. He saw the jars on the window.

'You shouldn't do that. Those things don't last forever, you have to be careful. Why didn't you leave them at the lab?'

'I thought they might lose them ... you know, admin errors ...'

They'd shown her the warehouse, tall towers containing countless drawers – something like the storage for those Arctic ice blocks, with their million-year-old clues. Sarah might not want to remember, but she didn't want her memories lost among those cavernous halls.

The late-night culture show was running a special on Naoko. Now twenty-five, she had been a prodigy discovered early on. She'd picked up a violin when she was two, practised twelve hours a day from the age of seven. Her work had been criticised as technically brilliant but emotionally cold, the presenter said. A camera closed in on the impassive face of Naoko as she performed.

Later she was interviewed. 'Do you regret not having time for a normal life, friends, relationships?'

'It's a sacrifice worth making. I would do anything for my music,' she spoke back in her quiet, emotionless voice. Sarah saw her sharp intense look and recognised her from the train. Sarah could not sleep that night, the bed was too huge. She padded out to the kitchen and retrieved the jars from the window-sill. She put them beside her pillow. They now gave off the scent of tarmac and old roses. They would have to go back in the fridge in the morning. Sarah returned to bed. The Cat had come in from the kitchen. She felt the shape and weight of him on her feet and she fell asleep.

It was late July and the raspberries had finally come out in the garden. The previous couple had sold the ground floor apartment to move somewhere with room for their new baby, but the canes remained. Sarah pushed a raspberry into her mouth, felt the hairy tension of its skin, the burst of mitigated sweetness on her tongue, joy with the undercurrent of something like regret.

She reached for the feeling, but she couldn't quite grasp it. She had the impression of something falling away, the Cat slipping out of an open window. She fled back into the house, making dusty footprints on the pristine tiles; she unlocked the fridge and looked in. There was a gap in the arrangements. One of the jars was gone.

Sarah searched for the printout to identify the lost jar, but the page was missing or mislaid. She wasn't good with paperwork these days. There was always something she couldn't put her hand on, an insurance document, medical receipt, the instructions for the boiler, things that ... Things that *he* would..? Things that *she* should ... Sarah tapped her head with her fingers three times as her chest tightened. She felt the scar on her temple. She was being stupid; they would have the details at the lab.

Back at the clinic in that nursery room Sarah noticed curtains patterned with elephants and giraffes. A baby's rattle was discarded on the floor. She'd returned merely to recover the paperwork but found herself face to face with the consultant. Sarah had brought a bag with her, there was a scent of tarmac, old roses and spilt milk.

Sarah explained what had happened, the information she wanted. 'We cannot supply the details of that particular file,' the consultant said.

She did not press him. The glass jars in the bag clinked against her thigh. 'Can you put the memories back in?' she asked.

'It's expensive. And, of course, one of the jars is missing,' he said, simply, in his white coat. He continued to explain. Replacing the memories wasn't as straightforward as their extraction; some of the links might have been lost. He tapped his fingers against the table. Sarah saw herself slipping through those white clothed arms, felt her thoughts falling like sleet, the pitter patter of cats, children, cats.

Back at home she went around the house opening cupboards and drawers, pulling out old files, tearing the place apart. The Cat meowed with hunger. She took him by the scruff of the neck and flung him into the yard. She reached into the darkest corners of the built-in wardrobe and pulled out a tie, smooth, a babygro, soft unworn.

'Something's gone wrong,' she said and pressed her fingers into her forehead, tapping.

Her brother came round as soon as she called. He let himself in with his spare key. In the hallway he found a string: *cat gut,* he thought.

Sarah was sitting in the dark. She had the tie and the babygro on the coffee table. Samuel wouldn't look at them.

'There was a young couple with a baby here before me,' Sarah said. Samuel nodded, watching the mouths moving on the muted television.

Sarah grabbed the remote and turned up the sound. A musician filled the screen.

'She's Naoko, that musical prodigy. They said her virtuosity left people cold.'

On the news report, they were calling her new album a sensation.

'She's not mechanical anymore,' said Samuel.

'Every time I hear this new music I cry.'

'Doesn't everyone? Isn't that what they're saying?'

'Not like this.' Sarah turned on the lamp. She'd cried so much, he could see the red blotches on her skin. 'I can't stop listening.' She pointed to the stereo.

Samuel put his hand to his face.

Sarah could feel the pattern of the sofa fabric under her fingers like Braille, she could feel the dip in the seat where someone heavier than her had sat before.

'Sarah, you were married ... you knew each other since you were twenty. His name was David.'

'Married?'

She looked around the quiet, contained sitting room.

'So we broke up ... just one of those things ...'

But Samuel's face: dismay, guilt, again that careful tenderness.

'There's more ... you had a ...'

He put his hands on her shoulders but she shrugged them away.

There was scratching at the door. Sarah got up to let in the Cat. She held him in her arms.

'The cat ...' Samuel explained, 'they said it would be a good idea ...'

Sarah shook her head. 'These are not mine,' she pointed to the tie and the babygro, 'take them away.'

As he left he could hear the music playing all over again.

There was a lunchtime concert at the local gallery. On the walls were depictions of lovers, mothers, war. Her brother came in late, flustered.

Naoko's bow moved across the strings. In Sarah's mind, tiny firings, her body shook, there was momentary static from the

36

amplifiers. People in the audience were crying. Naoko's face displayed tenderness, happiness, pain. Sarah recognised everything. She noted the small scar at Naoko's temple, a scrap of gingham in the pocket of her black shirt.

At the end of the performance, a man walked up to Naoko, looked into her eyes and kissed her. Sarah stood, blindly moving towards Naoko and her new lover. Samuel called out as he saw David's face. He put his arms tightly around his sister and led her away.

Flashes of Entropy and Hope

'I want to send you for tests,' said the doctor. Barbara turned round to look at him. She was buttoning up her blouse. He smiled and handed her an envelope.

At home she steamed it open. It was matter of fact. It did not say. This woman may be dying, please check. Neither did it mention the word, routine. This kind of thing happened all the time but it was not everyday.

Burgeoning buds, blousy blooms, everything was a reminder. The sun bled in, extra-intense. It was June but it had the maniacal heat of August; that last fling panic of sexed up, steamy fervour, low slung, sultry late night sunsets. She flung off her tops to put on lighter ones and that too was a reminder. She tried not to catch sight of herself in the mirror.

The sizzle had caught her daughter early too. She was fifteen. She was heading out with Eddie. Eddie who was seventeen and had a motor bike. Her daughter wore cut-off jeans and a crop top, everything cut off too soon. She was called Emily. She shook her long hair down her back like a shampoo advert and when she and Eddie held hands it was with the fingers interlocked, jammed together – the way they entwined their legs when side by side on the sofa watching TV programmes about young things who bit each other or flesh tearing zombies. They were taking the motorbike to get to the sea. They moved so fast out of the front door that their words were behind them, hanging in the hallway when they'd gone.

She had been worried about the motorbike. Boy racers. Emily regarded her with the patience cultivated for the old and imbecilic. 'Nothing bad will happen,' she said, swinging the spare helmet with her skinny wrists. 'We're all dying, all the time,' she thought the boy mumbled. It could have been that; he was seventeen, he had a goatee.

Later she followed them to the sea. Some sea, maybe not their one. What they said and where they went were necessarily two different things. She went to the place called Greystones, where there was no sand, only grit and shingle. She held weighty, sea softened stones in her hands then let them clatter onto the beach. She sat down and watched the sea creeping in, washing out, laid back with stars; she threw rocks at it, fled. She trod the harbour walk like a penitential pilgrim, she vanquished the hill in one breath, discarded it on the descent. She never looked back. She could feel the stares of pleasure trippers, strolling souls, hot on her hair. She made for the car. Young lovers embraced on a bench between the car park and the sea. She turned the key. She was still alive, the key was warm.

Lumps like pebbles in her breasts when the darkness finally fell; her husband asleep to the sound of her internal screaming. This time she watched her face in the mirror; the face of the possibly condemned. She seemed serene. You couldn't tell a thing from it. When Emily came home, her clothes intact, her breath hot and determined, her face too gave nothing away. Before bed, she had leaned against her mother on the sofa, her hair spilling over her mother's arm, her head nudging against the pain. She had brought her mother a stone, something like an agate, with a smooth edge; a worry stone for the edge of the thumb.

Eddie had driven away slowly, the dusk thickening his disappearance. He was a good boy. He kissed Emily on the cheek but kept his face there for the longest. Time was difficult to measure when running out. She'd stood back, in the holding bay of the hallway where she was not held or holding but she could hear the TV where her husband was watching and there was laughter. When Eddie stepped onto the driveway to go and they unclasped their hands she stepped out and asked him to post the referral letter on his way past the post box. If it was him who brought it sailing away into the darkness, all energy and zest, there might still be hope.

*

Emily and Eddie were baiting lightning on the quay, and it was forked. Across the bay the flashes lit up midnight townlands in isolated glimpses as if God with torches was looking for his keys in the eternal driveway. Here. There. This way a bit. Further back.

When the breeze still had air in it, they knew they were okay. They wore t-shirts and jeans and Emily felt the solid beam of his arm around the outside of hers. He felt the seam of her jeans against his thigh, he leaned down and kissed the edge of her hair. Her calves lick curl lifted, shook and died. When the thunder smothered them they knew they were chancing it. They kissed completely. At the end of the quay the wires crackled. All Emily wanted to do was swim, dive-bomb off the pier and sink in, watch the lightning experimentally dance on top of the water.

Eddie was leaving at the end of the summer. He was filled up with love for her; he just didn't know he had to do anything with it. She was loathe to count the days. Her Dali calendar was disgruntled by her apparent indifference. But there was a lot you could ascertain from the periphery. Time was flashing by.

If her father was the air traffic controller and her mum was the girl who delivered the sandwiches and coffee then she fell below the radar. Emily flipped the axis of 24/7 and slept in a honeyed bed, roamed the black night with confidence and fervour. But if it were the other way around and her mother was the mistress of flights and near misses then she was sussed and she strung out the summer with Eddie under the heavy lidded gaze of her mother's restless vigilance.

But they drank beer on the beach after dark. One of the lads, giant limbs, small head, acted the flasher for the whitehead bus tour sea front promenaders. He used hen party props, chocolate penises melting in the humidity. They collected tuts and shaking heads and the odd raucous cackle. They slid into clubs once in a while when the rain drove them inside. When midnight passed, in the tribal stomping, she lit up her phone and it was already August. Eddie was slouched in a corner on a slope of coats. She found his hand and she made him dance. There was no rain here only sweat, brine and coffee.

Emily found out she was epileptic on the dance floor. The strobe lighting sent her into a spinning fit, flit, flit; flashbacks of dream sequences and recent dalliances.

When she awoke she was cold, shudder huddling while the world switched on again, in portions, vision, feeling, sound. She had become a small creature at the bottom of a mountain of human concern. The dance music was still playing; drumbeat dissonance, out of time with the trotting of her heart.

Three weeks later the gang wanted to know if they were going to cut her brain in half. Someone else asked if that would make her schizophrenic. They were on the beach again and the nights came quicker now, her mother's shift had lengthened and the fact of epilepsy added a high note to her voice when she said 'see you later' to Emily. Across the bay the lighthouse spun, flashed, there, gone, there, gone.

Eddie was leaving tomorrow. Emily pressed into his biking leathers. He was going to take her for a drive somewhere but he hadn't decided yet. They were going to stay out all night. She didn't care. Her mother could jump. You only had one life and this was it.

They went into the mountains. The bike roared and so did the wind. Eddie sang something but the sound was swallowed whole. They paused for a view of the city, like stars they said; but the stars were meek in comparison. They went further until the string behind them broke; they went on like a prayer without rosary beads.

It was just them. Turned this way, at the crest there was no city. There was gorse, stones. They sat on granite. His-her hands found warm places. In his silence was the remembrance of his voice. In her stillness was the echo of her fervour. She drifted into him and thought it could be the epilepsy. He drunk her in and thought of nothing.

They saw flashes, out of the black; ripples of light, undulations snaking the sky. The aurora borealis this far south, they weren't meant to be there.

In the morning they went home, the cold in their bones and the light in their heads. Her father was up early on a ladder fixing the flashing. Her mother was drowning in coffee. She hadn't slept. Her fury was thunder and Emily felt it overhead. But all she could see were scenes, flashes of her and Eddie, on a beach, on a mountain, dancing like one person. Then him on his own, driving away till whenever.

*

Skim. The stone slipped across the top of the water. The sea was a battleship grey with a liver of cerulean, foaming at the lips its puckered kisses smacking on the shore. Dip, dip, the stone, flat and oval skudded across the ocean night, like a satellite on a far flung trajectory, unspun from orbit, now loosed across the dark matter heavens. Dropped.

Barbara took off her clothes. There was always a nip in October. Toes. They curled against the element of wind. Out on the promontory a man was walking his dog or wrestling a whale or hanging onto an umbrella, it was hard to tell. Rain spat and she tasted salt. The sea leapt and she drank of a spring. Because of everything before, her skin was crying.

Matthew couldn't touch her, at first for fear, then out of respect, then apropos of revulsion. That revulsion unsaid of course, caught in the gullet, closed in behind tight mealy-mouthed lips, an indigestion of horror. There are phases in intimacy aren't there? That amorphous amour from a distance, then the jasmine hint of possibility, then that full clothed shuddering, the turning inside out of velvet pockets, swan necks looping. Then there is the breath. Then there is the tuning on the shore, dark sand, the retreat, the furrow, the frown. And the froth ran backwards through the music of pebbles. And the sand hoped. Went dry. Would have wept, disintegrated.

They kept pieces of her in kidney dishes, wiped the scalpels clean. And Matthew held her as if he was very far away in history, as if she was in his past, a relic that turns to dust in the light. And back in their bed at night, she felt that kisses could have been glue.

She throws herself into the water. Skims across the frantic surface first. Dip. Dip. Her legs and arms are bare, the suit sagging, this shrivelled skin.

So cold. The foam folds round her body, smooth. The water is sloshing under her suit. Salt lingers on the wound, the ridge of it, like puckered shore shapes. And the tenderness of sea is the inverse of betrayal. How could he forget the press of their souls against one another, the kiss of affinity, the lapping of likeness, the mapping of cells that sung with recognition?

Her head is bare. As smooth as the stone.

She drops. Inside the water she is a whole thing, swims. And the pull of her limbs is the evidence of hope. And her skin wears the grit of the salt, grit, like her teeth when she thought she might die, when they sent the chemical elixir through her veins and it journeyed from the outside in. When she and he kept everything in, screams, protestations, that horror in a purse, turned at last frantically inside out. Where did I leave my pain?

Matthew couldn't find the words, the associations left him bereft. There was always that smell about her, the signature of decay. Betray, it's such a hefty accusation. He would not leave it at his own door. He remembered her dancing at the beginning; the Twist or something that caught her in his mind, spinning, unwinding, spinning again. He did not want to juxtapose the light of her with this. Amour inside armour. The back of the newspaper was always fascinating.

He wasn't a swimmer. Once or twice he had paddled with

their daughter Emily, his shins and ankles blindingly white and hairy. When she was two, she didn't like the way the sand at the shore stuck to her wet feet. She was forever trying to wash it off but when she came out of the sea it stuck on again. She sat in the foam and cried.

Barbara came out of the water, shook herself like a dog, hairless. The water rolled down the curve of her neck, it rolled into the dip at the top of her suit, kissed the place where her breasts had been. She was clean. The wind was the slice of a knife. The man with his dog was closer now, lifted his hand in a gracious salute. The sand on the edge of the shore was so dark and the foam rushing in was so white.

*

The man with the monobrow does the crossword. He holds his pen poised over the newspapers soft flesh. A hirsute man in a suit, astute. A knife of light slices the crossword – diagonally – not down or across. As a boy he would never step on shadows.

He left his wife this morning, now certifiably dying, crying in the arms of his sister-in-law. 'A little sniffle,' is what she'd said, her eyes white, the edges of her features dark pink like an inflamed wound. The tissue was crushed beyond utility.

He would never step on shadows but he let them wrap round him in the night when he stood star bathed in a rural village house's back garden. Eyes shut, arms outstretched, short trousers, aged eight, bare feet, rooted. He wanted to feel the turn of the earth.

The sun is rubberstamped on the horizon, turns gold from blood red. The wide water of Killiney Bay is lit as if with a million candles.

'I don't feel broken,' his wife had said. 'It's as if there isn't anything wrong. I can walk down the street to buy apples. I can hold them in my hand and feel their wax, their shield. I can press my thumb into the skin and bruise it. I can take a bite, clean and tangy. You know what I mean by that,' she said, pressing her thumb into his skin above the elbow, placing her hand against his newly shaven chin, just a small nick, that stung. 'When the sun shines on my head, my hair gets warm and I feel good. But inside I'm being eaten up and later I go home and take a nap all of a sudden like I used to do when expecting the children.' The sleep with no undoing.

His car was also kaput, hence the commute, the battery on his mobile phone was ailing. The train clung to the cliff above the bay and he had always wanted to sail down such a sky in a parachute, to chuck himself out into fear.

In Oncology, unmasked, much later in the day, he strode out of Surgery to meet the relatives of his patient. Irony had faint humour. He feigned empathy as he had done all the years to stem the flow of their tears, to shore up their devastation. He indicated in nods and in the press of his firm tips that he was to be depended upon, even when there was nothing he could do. Then he fled, with solid careful steps.

He wasn't the kind of man to hold his head in his hands, but his wife had framed his face with her fingers, then entwined her fingers with his. 'You,' she said, 'you,' and of the radio 'I love this song.' And then she undid her fingers and he had the sensation of falling backwards and falling and falling. At that moment neither of them was scared.

Bog Body

All that summer she long jumped over wide gaps in the harvested bog. There was nothing to do. Her skin was a vessel for the sun, a honeycomb of cells filled with nectar, the throbbing of insects, the humming of bees.

She begins a good way back. She can usually find some sort of a clear run, bar the odd rogue heather. She feels the prickle of dried grass and lichen against her bare feet as she makes her precipitous approach to the bank edge. She launches her body as a missile into the air. It cuts through the shimmering heat, making it warp and buckle. Then, in the slicing of time she is held, suspended, over the watery hollow, its cool pools pressed against the dank muddy cheeks of black turf. Then she is over – five or six feet across – coming to rest on pointed toes; her breath hitting the back of her lungs; her muscles slackening until her heels drop to earth, her thin arms dangling by her sides.

It is August, a round bellied month, slow with heaviness and heat. She sees them coming – three local boys – stocky trolls with thick wrists and necks, square pallid faces and muddy eyes. She recognises them from school. They lumber across the bog in her direction.

She watches them move with the same slow nonchalance as cattle, the same resignation. She remembers that first day, her introduction to the class – the bright kindly faces of black haired girls with boyish crew-cuts, cheeky freckle faced siblings suppressing smirks. And them, a solid bulk of muddy eyed menace; their arms resolutely folded; their mass stretched across the back wall of the classroom like a buttress against outside forces. Now they heave themselves out of hollows, step between hummocks. One stumbles over a piece of bog deal wedged into the ground. He gives it a mean sideways kick, sending splinters spraying. She's afraid they are bored.

Tick, tick, tick go water crickets lazy in the heat. In the school yard, the boys lean against the low stone wall that marks the periphery, beyond which nettles and brambles thrive. The girls approach her, hesitant, demonstrating an alien game where there are four corners and the fifth person is somehow the odd one out. She stands, uncertain in the centre, unsure if she is in or is already excluded. Confusion overwhelms her, she retreats into a space, a kind of dip between the yard and the back wall of the school, a runoff where the water gushes in damp weather. She pulls back lank wisps of pale hair from in front of her eyes and twists chewed ends around her index finger.

Across the yard she can hear the boys mutter, they travel between breakaway groups of tag and spies spreading Chinese whispers. She stands, twisting her foot into the dust and sees the children of her age laugh and turn away. Only the younger ones – tumbleweed sized bundles with rolling shoulders – remain. They hold the pleats of her cotton dress, its exotic pinks and reds the only flashes of colour among their more serviceable clothing, their faded denim and unravelling cord trousers. She is a butterfly that has come unexpectedly among them. When the bell rings they chase her to the classroom door then let her go.

Behind the teacher's head are tall windows, through which the sun comes blindingly in the mornings, carving lemon meringue slices into the dark oak desks with their obsolete inkwells and blackened grooves dug out with HB pencils. She watches the slow parade of cotton wool cumulus against the sapphire sky and feels the words 'out there.'

The repetitive drone of spellings and tables stagnates the air. Under her chair and down at the small of her back is the gradual accumulation of tiny rolled up balls of paper; the punctuation of the afternoon's slow unfurling. She feels the pip of another missile, hears a snigger covered under the rustling of pages. The teachers raises her voice, says her name. She has been asked a question. She cannot bluff it. Her mind is at the back wall, being

47

rolled in the plump palm of the Ringleader. She hears a clap, hands slapped together. She is sent into the corner on the raised dais beside the teacher's desk. She sees them in her periphery, their faces jolly, their shoulders shaking with mirth. She rocks from her round solid heel onto the ball of her foot. From time to time she lifts and balances on her toes, staring at the wood panel, ready to dance or fly. Somewhere else. A fly ricochets against the window and drops to the floor beside her, his thread legs flailing.

Now the heat of the bog radiates into her feet. She waits. She sees them, the boys from school, pick their way across the adjacent sawn out banks where turf is footed and stands to attention in three-sided spires. She is poised, like a hare, tendons on a spring, tightly coiled. They reach her now, roll to a stop, a wall of weatherworn boulders. The Ringleader is broad, block solid, his lips the colour of crushed blackberries, swollen like the fruit.

'What are you doing?' he asks.

'Jumping,' she says, the soft tones of her blow-in accent lightening the initial vowel, giving the impression of weightless flight.

'Jumping,' repeats the Sidekick, the emphasis on the middle consonants, making the word heavy, indicating somehow, the thud of landing.

The third boy, the Follower, laughs. He has the nose of a fox, the keen bright eye and wiry build of a hound. They say more then, between each other. She can't pick it up, her ears are attuned to a different pitch. They wait for an answer, she doesn't know the question. They are insulted, she thinks herself too good. She tries smiling but that too seems to be a foreign dialect, they think themselves mocked. She recognises their sullen stirrings, like a stick in quicksand. She sees a sprig of yellow tormentil, tiny but tenacious, trailing over a rock. She says something to them, about the heat, or the holidays. The softer her voice becomes, rustling like rushes, the more it angers them.

The sun, devoid of malice soaks into all of them, gently.

They move towards her, a resolute collective. She doesn't resist. She has anticipated this moment in her stomach's mutinous churnings on school day mornings, the reckless thudding of her fist-enclosed heart. It had to happen. They scoop her up in their shovel hands, hold her aloft between them. Like pallbearers they struggle and stumble over the rough grass, their faces contorting with exertion, their teeth clamped together. She is clasped by one around the legs, by another around the middle, just below her straining ribs, his hand resting on her solar plexus. Then finally, by the Ringleader, around her long flimsy neck, fright visible in the throbbing of veins under her thin skin.

They descend into the watery hollow into which she never fell while jumping. She sees a dragonfly arc above her, tracing the path of her exquisite flight. She smells the stewing soil, fibrous yet yielding. For a moment she loves it.

They feed her, face down, into the bog. Into her mouth and nostrils swill the bogs rank ale. She tastes its foul decay: dead wood, the remains of crawling, creeping things, luminescent moss, pungent fungus, gelatinous lichen. Above her, as they heave and tussle, their forms obliterate the sun, bathing her in heavy shadow. They work methodically, with industry and intent, the nod and murmur of well rehearsed practise, the culling of poultry, the dipping of sheep.

Through time she feels the weight of the bog, the strata of eons pressing upon her, the thin prehistoric cries of the ritually slain, outcasts and villains. She becomes accustomed to the taste of iron. In dusky evenings, after the sun slips behind round honey-crested hills, long dark shadows finger-paint her resting place. The corncrake skulks in the sedge, guarding secrets. In the languorous night she dreams, endlessly impeded journeys, horrific stagnation.

She waits. She watches the world, glassy eyed, under a film of brown water brimming with the once living. Seasons come and go, summers under the weight of unrelenting mist, clear January's, stormy Octobers. Other children grow, form and disband alliances, fatten up, slim down, stretch out, laugh, play, fight, love, win, lose.

She waits. The oblong leaved sundew innocently unfurls its bright white flowers, its spoon shaped leaves with glistening red tentacles. It lures all manner of foul creatures: flies, midges, beetles and ants into its mucilaginous secretion, dissolves its struggling victims, then digests them. She bides her time. She dreams of osmosis, creeping advancement.

Years into the future, she wrenches herself out of the sucking bog, its desperate mouth fastened round her, the squelch and pop as it releases her like regurgitation. Under the earth she stretched her fragile fingers against the immovable soil, made of living remains but dead, dead weight. Everything she could not do. Now she pushes out, presses her fingerprints against the sagging soggy earth, she makes her mark. The bog bounces back, erases her. She rises up, a ragged mast on the high sea, weather-whipped and pliant. Under her tanned leathery skin, her bones are frail, a luminescent lattice, roped loosely by sinew. She feels the wind behind her, filling up her sails, she readies herself for flight. Above her head a heron makes determined for hill-framed shining water.

She leaps light-footed from the hollow. Moths rise with her. Into the far distance bog cotton waves like tiny flags of surrender. The ground propels her bounding steps. The end of the bog is marked by three stones with lichen faces, their mouths in startled ohs, their eyes fixed and staring towards the wide gap in the bog. Her clod pressed ears catch the laughter of still undiscovered beings suspended in the soil.

She lays her hands upon them, three stone heads. She feels their pitted resistance at her rough fingertips, ignores it. She begins, one by one to rock them gently forwards and back, back and forth, until the strongly woven moss loosens at their base, its fibres tearing apart. They stand, like the teeth of diseased gums, dislodged and wavering. Her crushed core ignites. Crackling and spitting she hurls the rocks down the springy slope where they lurch and judder. At the edge of the bank they languish, expressions contorted. She gives them one last, considered, benign, smile then drops them into black water, sees them sink and disappear.

She roams now, like a wild animal over rock castles and her hair, once pale, is copper, plaited and matted like a Rastafarian, a sweat shirt tied round her middle under her new breasts, her legs the colour of honey and dung, laddered with old blood. She long jumps out of the bog, springing from a rainbow mosaic of sphagnum moss, to a long wide bank of solid ground. From there she climbs the honey crested hill, higher and higher, along ridges swathed with sedge where the wild air makes it ripple like waves. Her ears fill with the euphoric whoosh of wind and water. From here she can see beyond closed valleys into the rest of the world. There is colour, space and light, different people. She opens her winged limbs and waits for the gust that will lift her into the distance. She whoops.

Gods and Other People

'Step away,' said the Policeman. 'Step away from the life.'

'Goddarn it,' I said, dropping the girl's limp wrist and swallowing the breath of life so quickly it gave me indigestion. I was just giving her a second chance. She was a beautiful girl, that sacred age, hovering between nineteen and twenty. Fucking unfulfilled potential. Her long soft hair spilling out all around her head. The pills spilling out of her fingers into a little molehill on the floor. You could have sworn she was going to make it. Her lips were still warm.

'Step away,' he said again, although his face was obscured by the crash helmet – dark blue with an opaque visor – and the iron in his voice was muffled. I wasn't going to argue. That's a given. You don't.

I'd been trying to revive the girl even though she was technically dead. I don't see what all the fuss is about; they do it all the time in A&E on the Ground. I heard of one guy who was revived after an hour and was sitting up in bed chatting soon after.

I needed to wash my hands. I indicated my intention to the Policeman. He understood. Godliness is next to cleanliness. It's non-negotiable. I scrub under my armpits every morning. I have a bidet for Christ's sake. I wash my feet every night before I lay down to rest if there isn't anyone offering to do it for me.

I went over to the small sink in the corner of the room. The girl lived in a bedsit – pleasant enough, good views – but with a general ground in grottiness. The usual: cooker, fridge, armchair, bed, filthy curtains. It was not so much the incontrovertibility of having to shag and eat in the same space – I'm not surmising here, she'd had a boyfriend. That's what it was all about. He was the one and only. He left her. She thought it was the end of the world and then made it so. The problem with the bedsit was the residue: all the DNA in the dried snot, the hair, the fingernails, the skin flakes that had got into the carpet, building up layer on layer, until it was singing with human electric and I tell you, that buzzes on my radar, makes my skin giddy and my temperament itch.

I put the plug in and filled the sink. I washed my hands properly, rubbing into the crevices between the fingers, the back of the hands, past the wrists; I even had a go under my finger nails. Then I did the palm, the back of the hand and the fingers up to the tips. The whole process, says the hand washing directive, should not take less than two minutes. She had that dainty lavender soap. It's meant to be calming but to be honest there's nothing more chilled out than being dead.

I was feeling anything but relaxed. I put my hands up to my face and sniffed them. I smelled of her. Sweet thing; perfect in every way, apart from the missing breath.

I used to use that stuff – coal tar – until they didn't make it anymore. I used to like the way the mortals gave a little sniff and screwed up their noses even though they didn't know anyone was there. Like this girl would have done, given the chance, but she was too far gone by the time I got there, drifted away on a sea of pills. It was a shame. That's where it gets me, the sense of irony. She didn't know that the next day she was gonna get a letter offering her a new job in Canada where she would have met Mike, an ex mechanic self made successful entrepreneur with a love of nature and a warm hearted personality. Those bloody astral postmen blow it every time. They're supposed to see to it that the important stuff gets through: the life changing messages. Of course, every so often they get a directive from Head Office to lose a letter down the back of a cabinet, give someone an experience that will create backbone or appreciation but sometimes they just mess up. And it's the likes of me that are left picking up the pieces.

I was really disappointed I hadn't come through for her. I've done this thing quite a few times and never had a Policeman show up on me before. I guess when the people upstairs say that someone's dead, they're supposed to be the ultimate authority. They will always get you on a technicality. It's like the way the argument goes for abortion. You ask, 'when does life becomes life?' It's a tough call. Are you gonna point your finger at a continuum and say tada! that's the moment things begin. Are you going to say it's the same for each and every one of us when nothing ever is?

So, similarly, you ask 'when is a death a death?' I like to err on the side of caution, generosity even. I like to say dead's not dead till the spirit leaves the room. I'm a rugby player; the game is still on till you kick it into touch. And I'm a tall guy; if you want me to leap into the air and field that spirit before it goes out through the roof then I will oblige. I will do it. I will take that golden translucent orb and I will tuck it in under my arm and I will go for that try.

You have to touch but only briefly. You don't want to zap them with the intensity of your godliness, burn their synapses just by looking. I'm not saying I haven't made mistakes in my time. You have to use a sort of gentle optimism. That sense of spring thawing frost. Don't overkill – so to speak.

When it was obvious I'd finished washing, the Policeman came and stood in front of me. He handed me a silk handkerchief out of his uniform pocket so that I could dry my hands. 'I'm going to have to take you in,' he said in a relatively kindly monotone, 'checks and balances,' he said, 'internal auditing.'

'My internals don't need auditing,' I said. But it was too late. He had me in the straitjacket before I exhaled.

I've been through this so many times before. It's why I keep my head shaved. It's easier for them to get the sticky electrode pads on while they show me all kinds of stimuli, including playbacks of my transgressions. Most of the time they are checking for my moral reaction rather than the physical stuff. They zoom in on my judgement circuits, test the connection between the cortex and the amygdala. They are looking for evidence of guilt, not truth, not whether I've done something or not – they know most of that already – but how I feel about it, whether there's a yowl in my soul or not.

Then they put me in the MRI scanner for two hours. No problem. I can keep still for decades if it's required of me. To pass the time I watched re-runs of the all the great rugby games in my head. Got a mental red pen and circled the 'what ifs' and 'almosts' on the path to sporting glory.

I thought about the nearly guys, the missed kick, the dropped ball and whether I would intervene or not. But you know, so much depends upon the individual. We have this free will gig going you know. There's a lot of tough guys out there, they take the knocks and they move on. But some never really get it together after they fumble the winning score. You have to ask yourself what the knock on effect could be; would the 'Hand of God' have hooked him a multimillion dollar franchise, or make him leave his wife. It's a lottery really and it's a bit technical, a bit tricky. That's why we usually hire in the Legals on that and their mascot the Good Luck Fairy. Throw a bit of shamrock into the mix and a pot of gold and you are steaming.

But I'm blabbing here and that's one thing that really gets my goat, gods who do all the talking and never listen. I mean surely that's a prerequisite of the job. Listen to your clients. That's all they really want. The rest is negotiable. They may think they may want a Georgian mansion in the country with four acres and its own orchard. You can nod and look serious for quite some time but in the end you just hand them a townhouse in a happening city because you know it's better for them. Some of those gods are way too soft; *be careful what you wish for*, have they never heard of that? They give people what they want and make them twice as unhappy. They don't get away with it now though, not with all this Scrutiny. Several of them have been demoted to genie in the past couple of year for minor misdemeanours and as for the ones that really screwed up, well, we don't like to ask.

When they finished with the MRI, they slid me out. I was chilled out and maybe a little cocky. 'You've only seen what's in my head,' I said. 'How about what's in my heart?'

Having open heart surgery while you're awake is an absolute riot. Not. It's not so much the Pain and Anxiety it's seeing the look on their faces when they peer in. It's a bit too full on even for them. I mean the heart has its own memory and we're talking eons here; well in the case of me being one of the higher powers, the heart imprints are pretty heavy; everything you felt for centuries, heartache, despair, love of course, the beauty thing, cupid and violins, desolation and regret, the squalor of the soul. Heart. Rending. There's stuff that's just so personal they know they shouldn't be looking at it, like a mama reading her schoolgirl daughter's diary when she's just discovered the joys of heavy petting. Or no, that's crude. God, the girls, the girls get me every time, the way everything tears at their feelings, the looks, the glances, the idle comments, you may as well get their heart out on the block and beat it tender like a steak. You could nibble it raw and it would make you cry.

I was lying back on the trolley checking my fingernails when they said 'If you really want to care for people we're going to give you what you want.' Uh oh. What was I saying earlier about people's dreams coming true? Sometimes it's the worst thing that can have ever happen. Lottery winners stalked by worthy causes, weirdos, maniac relations, guilt and self-doubt. Hell on earth. Sometimes the cruellest thing you can do to someone is answer their prayers.

In many ways being male is like being stuck between a rock and a hard place. Becoming a woman-god seemed to be altogether more accommodating. Losing my Jean Genie was a wrench but getting a built-in incubation room in my belly was a top phenomenon. And there was something in it.

Yeah, I kind of felt nostalgia for the guy I'd been so into before but had now cast aside. Besides, all I could really think about now was the kid, I mean my child, the one that was growing inside me. Yes, they'd given me that as well. It already had blobby hands and a fishy kind of face. It already looked somewhat like me. When I played music I knew he was (he, it just happened to be a he, I was sure) would strum along on his amniotic guitar, in his lava lamp womb with the drumbeat thud of my heart in his ears.

Meat is best cooked slowly. It took 9 months and my heart was tenderized beyond belief. I wasn't prepared for the pain. The inverse of a thousand orgasms. But the boy wasn't budging. Didn't he know how much I wanted him? They said there would have to be a C-section. The humans would have to intervene to retrieve him. Don't say it. Don't even give me a whiff of the irony.

But he came out, strong, smacking the world in the jaw, bellowing. Gorilla boy, beating his chest. And then the room went quiet. 'There's another one, they said' as they swallowed their fear. She came out as silent as the ....well ... you know what and as blue as a bird's egg.

'You knew this,' I shouted, my voice high and what would have been known in the poker rooms of the soul as hysterical. 'You know everything. Why didn't you tell me?'

Fucking medical science. I'd even whispered in the ears of some of these guys in their sleep or rather their predecessors more than half a century ago, put them onto that whole ultrasound thing. I gave them this amazing advance – the ability to take a picture of the insides, and then a photograph of the housesitter when he's still spaced out on life and doesn't know he's there yet.

The boys upstairs must have got a kick from the tumescence of their ingenuity. They had wanted to teach me a lesson. The midwife had my daughter, turning stone cold and I couldn't do anything. I was too weak. I was cut in half on the table with my insides turned out. Kiss of life, goddamit. A kiss was everything I wanted to give her.

I had to leave it to the humans.

I couldn't see what was going on, my heart was thumping in

my ears and their frantic whispers were a cloak that I couldn't peer through. I tried to sit up but they pinned me down again. The surgeon started sewing me back together. I could see the reflection of my wound in the surgical lights.

Her whole life flashed before me. Ironic knife. And I knew that when they cut the umbilical cord they then tied it to your heart. First smile, first words, first steps, your finger held tight in their fist, soft cuddles, amorphous skin, holding them so close you would put them back inside you, the sup sup contented sup of milk their downy heads against your breast. Only now did I really understand breasts! And then they grow, engaging, inquisitive, sassy, infuriating, courageous, forever going away. And your love just gets bigger and bigger, following the widening space. I was her mother, I made her. I saw everything she could be right down to the bit where I leaned on her, frail in my old age. Because mortality was another gift they'd given me. And a big bite of the apple out of Eden. And it was only now that I got why it was Eve had to show Adam what life was really all about and women have being trying to do that ever since.

I just thought everything would be alright. I was high on the hormones, on being a human. But the midwife gave a little sob. She put my baby girl down, just for a moment and then I knew. She was gone. The room went dead. The nurse stopped sewing me up. She stood there with a needle held in the air and this black thread coming out of it, stretching all the way down, to me. Was there any point in putting me back together? The boy was howling as if he knew.

Then I saw him, the tall guy with the clean hands and bright hair. He crossed the room with his kit bag as if he was preparing for a game. He laid a finger on her. Just one. And he looked into her eyes. I knew the routine. And he blew, so gently across her face. The others couldn't see him; that was obvious. The midwife had a tissue, the consultant was knocking the hell out of the floor with the soles of his Italian leather shoes, gearing up to say something. There was another nurse holding the boy an inch from my face. I couldn't take my eyes off the guy, like I was his mentor and I wanted him to see him do it right. And he did. The sweetest sound I ever heard in my life was this tiny cry that got louder and louder and rang round the walls.

The guy slipped away, head bent, his mouth lifting slightly at the edges. Was he a maverick, like I had been? They'd given me her life and now I'd be waiting, watching out of the corner of my eye, down all the short years to see if they were going to take it back. Because life is not a game, they want you to know that. And there's always a trick in forgiveness.

Meringue

There was an angel at the end of the bed, she insists.

'Did you see it, when you came in?' she asks me, her thumb pressing fiercely into the back of my grasped hand, almost parting the metatarsals. I look down at her small white mop of a head. How is it she grows tinier every day but is taking so long to disappear?

'Did you see it?' She asks me again, agitated.

That's the words the nurses have for it. 'She was very agitated yesterday evening,' they tell me. It's like a code. They had to give her something, they say, to get her settled. No wonder she is seeing angels, between the drugs and the bags of marshmallows they hand out. Nice and easy to eat, they say, what with the sores on her mouth and the decrepit dentures.

Sugar rush, I say. Wired. One of the day's high points. Like Sasha and Natalie after a birthday party. I used to have to make them run around the garden fifteen times when they came home or they'd tear the heads off their Barbie dolls or send the dog loolah by tying one of my bras to its tail, usually one of the lacy ones which the dog then destroyed or embarrassed me with by leaving it in the next door's garden. There's no mistaking my bras, it's double d or die with me. Wouldn't go near those girls, though. They're all grown up now but they're like knitting needles. Went through that whole bulimia thing with Sasha a couple of years back. She swears she's stopped now but ... mmm those marshmallows do look tasty.

'Can you hear me?' Mama asks.

She's picked that up from people saying it to her. They all think she's deaf but she's always been like that. She only bothered to listen if you were deemed free of transgression. Forget X-Factor. Try guilt factor. Search and destroy self-esteem.

Don't get me wrong, I'm not hung up about it, haven't gone the counselling route either. I am the enlightened consumer of self-help books. *'Eleven steps to self-esteem', 'Turn on the light for the child within'. 'Don't get sad, beat your old folks round the head with a hockey stick.'* Just kidding on the last one.

'I hear you.' I say to my dear old Mama. 'But I didn't see anything.'

I don't usually pay much attention, I find it easier to block out the extraneous (sounds like a medical condition) mad goings on in the world today. I can't count how many times one of the girls has said to me, 'Did you see those guys in the park? They were dealing,' when all I saw was the sun resting gently on the grass and a cocker spaniel christening a row of silver birch. Or that one time a lady's purse was snatched, right next to me on the 25A to Chapelizod.

'Did you see anything?' the lady said. 'Did you see where the guy got off?'

Not at all. I was wondering if I'd missed the final of Britain's Got Talent and whether I'd be able to stop myself from lurching backwards if I got up and pressed the button before my stop.

'You ought to stand up straight,' Mama rants, twisting my hand until all the blood goes out of it. 'You're like the Hunchback of Nutter Damn, looking at the floor all the time ... I warned you,' she says, 'I told you you'd never hold onto a man that way.'

When you visit the very old, as you know, the same conversations come round and round like rolling news on the BBC. 'Whatever happened to Uncle Marcus, did he ever give up the drink? 'Did I ever tell you about the time I cut off all my hair and left it down the back of the settee?' And her absolute favourite 'No man leaves you at the altar without a good reason, you must have done something.'

Well it wasn't actually at the altar. It was two weeks before. As it happens, I was trying on my wedding dress, the dressmaker had managed to let it out another two inches and I was just making sure I could get it on. I was looking in the full length mirror and lifting up my head (for once, to minimize the resting chin syndrome) and I was thinking 'Meringue' and it was a light, gooey, happy feeling because I like meringue and I could see myself floating in a sweet, sugary, angelic cloud down the aisle of St Judes, and landing precisely in pump encased plump feet beside darling Richard, my own, finally, all six foot two of him and that's high not wide.

Everything felt just so and the cherry blossom had just come out and the street sweeper had been down earlier and sucked up all the cigarette butts and ripped crisp packets into its metal belly. The light was still lemon young, resting shyly on the tops of things, the houses opposite, the roof of the abandoned Fiesta in front of number 24. Shy the way you're supposed to be when you're not babe material (unless you mean that film with the pig in it) and the man you've fallen head over comfortable-walking-shoes in love with passes your cubicle on his way to the water cooler. Shy the way you're not supposed to pop up from behind the divider and ask him if he wants to go bowling next Tuesday. And then on Tuesday ask him if he's seen the remake of that classic 1970s sci-fi everybody's talking about and so on and so on it went until we were both well past shy and motoring before it got a chance to put the clamp on us.

So this morning I'm talking about. Everything felt just so. Absolutely. I could hear Sasha tearing up the stairs as usual. She does it a hundred times a day religiously. Stairway to Slim Heaven. She's supposed to go back down again but she burst in, barely puffed.

'Hey you look great,' she said, very convincing.

She is a sweetheart, like her mother was. Sweet eighteen, ready for the off. She'll be okay. At least I've done everything I could to stop her world from shattering completely. Thin ice.

She held out the mobile handset.

'It's Richard,' she said. 'Wants to have a word.' And her voice was round with giggles and optimistic as if she was still four and nothing bad had happened to her mum, my lovely big sister.

Richard was very apologetic in a formal kind of way, as if he was ringing up to cancel a cheque or a provisional holiday booking. You think you'd remember such a momentous phone call in detail but when I try to get a handle on it all I can think of are vague words like Regret, Inconvenience, Unable.

When I put the phone down, I just kept thinking meringue, meringue. But it was a different kind of meringue; a meringue puffed up and expanded, doing the job of polyfilla, filling the hole of a gaping Why?

Mama is getting impatient. 'I don't want to spend the rest of my life waiting for you to stop chewing.'

I cannot believe that she's ninety. Forty-five she was when she had me as an afterthought or before she fought my Dad off with the reinforced knickers and the garlic capsules. Now I'm forty-five, just like she was and just like Suzie was too when it happened, so it all adds up doesn't it, multiplies by a factor of two?

Two who? Just the two of us, Richard and me, cleaved apart by the forces of inertia. He wasn't really sure if he wanted to trade in BBC4 for the Living Channel or eau de reheated casserole for rose water and ylang ylang.

Or just the two of us, Mama and me, factors of each other, factoring each other into our otherwise non-eventful lives. Well non-eventful is better than us holding both ends of a disintegrating phone line while I have to tell her that Suzie has killed herself and yes, she's dead, really dead and I don't know anything else and I don't know why (unless what happened with David hit her harder than we realised). And I don't know how those two beautiful little girls are going to do without her and I don't know why it was her, not me, when she was so much better, in every way, than I am. And you knew that, didn't you Mama? Told me that a thousand disheartening times.

Or the two of us, Suzie and Rosie, I don't know what else to say. She was just my big sister, fabulous, an angel, just so composed and forgiving and generous and dead. Pale white,

white with the glory washed out in the blue light of the morgue. Blue eyes, blue lips, blue veins. In school they said 'remember veins is like the French word venir, to come'. The veins returning blood back to the heart for air.

Mama is on her way to the morgue but she's taking her time getting there. Has she forgotten what she asked me? I have. But she doesn't give in.

'The angel said he'd give you another chance,' she says.

A chance to live my life over? Why would I want that? I had my man, even if it was for just a little while and it was me he wanted, the bulk of me, the dimples where dimples shouldn't be, the sweat and the tears and the tablespoon of chilli in the bolognaise sauce. I had my children, well sort of, borrowed from Suzie until they were old enough to do without both of us. And they are fine, I can feel it, so I haven't slipped up there.

My hand is starting to get cold; she's holding it so tight. I let go on pretence of smoothing the bedclothes. I ask her if she wants her pillows straightened up. She mutters into her chin while I am doing it, worries the blanket hem between fingers as brittle as twigs. I have passed forty I am thinking, I am over the hill and bottom-shuffling down the other side on a cushion of rolling, unruly flesh. And every now and then I get a tweak or an ache only it never goes away, never quite heals and my frown lines are like the gouges between the slices of a takeaway pizza. I look at my Mama with her chicken neck and her rheumy eyes and I wonder how it's possible to be ninety, another lifetime again of falling apart. How is it that her powdery skin doesn't just crumple away like Wensleydale; her frail bones collapse all at once; and the eyes that have burned forever snuff out, trailing wisps of toxic smoke?

'You must have done something,' she persists, 'for him to up and leave you like that, no warning.' She leans forward.

I don't know why the blunt needle of her memory has her stuck in this particular groove on this run of the mill Monday.

Maybe she misses Richard; he used to pop in with me at the weekends. Perhaps it's all to do with the familiar, perhaps because she's had to skip her usual routine, she's jumped into the next track on the LP – (does she know they don't make them anymore?)

Maybe she's still annoyed at herself for letting our Dad give her the slip.

'Just popping out for the Sunday paper, want anything?' he said. He never came back.

Had a heart attack in front of the chippers at the age of 56. Never apologised or anything.

'Are you with me?' she says. She is staring at the foot of the bed. 'Leaving those two young girls; his own flesh and blood. He was a great man, a lovely father,' she continues.

'Yes, I'm with you Mama.' Blind man's bluff. Who am I reaching out to? 'Are you thinking about Dad?' I gamble.

I take her hand again but she pulls it away, makes it into a fist and slams it down on the covers. I think of making a fist too or rather of cramming fistfuls of marshmallows into my mouth. I can picture myself with pink and white squidgy cubes falling out of a gaping tunnel in the middle of my mountainous face.

'I don't believe all that about another woman,' she continues, directing her thoughts to the bedstead. Her voice has a pitch in it that makes my insides feel like a noodle dish that is being gathered up and eaten with chopsticks. It's the sound of a car in the wrong gear at a driving test, an excruciating whine that means you've failed.

She's confused. 'You must have driven him away, Suzie. David never would have gone otherwise. You never could get anything right, not like Rosie and now you see what you've done to her, saddled her with two teenagers and scared off poor Richard. Such a lovely man, Richard was.'

Mama sinks right back into the pillows, and they billow up around her like marshmallows. Or meringue. She is tired now and her eyelids start to lower like the metal tambours on shopfronts when you still want to look into them because there is something inside that you might want to buy but you just want to check first if the item is what you think it is and if the price is what you are willing to pay.

And when her eyes are closed, I keep sitting there and I look at her now that I can and I wonder how it is that Mama, Suzie, me and the girls so carelessly lost all our men and are left here waiting and watching, all except Suzie that is, well maybe Suzie is waiting and watching too.

And is it possible that all along Suzie thought that I was the good one?

The next time I visit, Mama is lying there, just the same, as if I had only slipped out for a minute.

They take me aside. They say it won't be long now, until she passes over. That's another one of their code phrases. You need to be on the ball if they say she's gone to sleep or to a better place. Don't assume anything, listen for further qualifiers.

I put my head up to her face and she is still breathing. She seems peaceful. Now I have begun to speak in euphemisms too, as if my mouth is full of something soft and sweet and sticky. I wonder how she can still be alive at ninety, how she must have had the antidote to the poison she carried round in her all those years. And as I think those thoughts something surges in her and she rouses from the deepest of sleeps. Her face creases with horror as she realises where she is, that this is the life she is still living. I move over to her and stroke her brow and the side of her head close to the departing hairline. I stroke her back to sleep as if she is an infant, plump with innocence and pleasure.

As she retreats into sleep, she searches for my hand but her fingers only skim over the end of ice-cold digits.

'I've just remembered, Rosie,' she whispers into the encroaching dark. 'Suzie said that if anything happened to her, you'd be there to look over them.'

And I did Suzie, I did my best and now they don't need me

anymore and neither does Richard. Now there's only you left Mama.

I take one more look at her, scraps and sticks. I won't ever leave her. If she needs me, the nurses will tell her that I merely stepped into the next room.

When I return there is angel at the foot of her bed.

'Can you see it?' she asks me, her breath running out.

'Are there any marshmallows left?' she wonders, rambling. 'Help yourself, Rosie. Help yourself.' I shake my head but she doesn't notice.

Her face becomes bright, her features smoothing out like pouring sand. She almost rises from her bed, leans on one robust elbow. 'You must see her,' she says, 'she's lovely, all dressed in white. I think I can hear her wings swishing.'

'I can see her now,' I say.

'Don't go away,' she whispers.

'I won't,' I tell her.

I stand watching over her as the lemon light filters into the room and rests on everything. I pivot and swish. 'Meringue,' I think. 'Meringue, Meringue, Meringue.'

Sad About the Plumber's Uncle

It wasn't the first time I'd called them and it wasn't the first time they hadn't shown up. I understand that there must be some hierarchy of need, aka Maslow, that plumbers go by. For example, Mrs. Brown is pushing eighty, she's knee deep in water, and her boiler has just blown up. Jill Ryan has an aspirational need for a massage and steam shower that will fit in with the way she sees herself. Survival versus Self-actualisation. I assume – I hope I'm not being naive here – that Mrs. Brown will be right at the top of the list, the A1 emergency for A1 plumbers, and that Jill Ryan's trim body will have to wait for its luxury sluice.

As for the rest of us, I can't tell you if a problem with the underfloor heating comes before a lack of pressure in the power shower. Where should I demand to be slotted? And where would they tell me I should be slotted if I tried to climb above my allotted ranking?

In my case, it was a leak. Somewhere in the upstairs bathroom, the family bathroom with separate walk-in-shower, double-ended bath and Spanish porcelain tiles. I had noticed a pool of water which my small son, Adam, emphatically denied creating. It was when I saw a stain the size of an eggcup on the living room ceiling that I began to panic. And of course, Denis was away on one of his long-haul trips to China, not that he would have had a clue anyway, not like Sandra Brennan's husband who does it all himself, logs on to those on-line forums to get tips from real trades people. He certainly knows his washers from his O rings.

'Call the professionals,' Denis said, when he rang from the other side of the world. 'Get it sorted asap.' Sometimes I think he forgets he's not *my* team leader.

I had been expecting the plumbers at two. This was my second attempt to lure them to my suburban, little bit upmarket four bed home. The first time the kids had been screaming in the background. Adam had been using his little sister's Sarah's nappy filling baby doll as a target for his new bow and arrow set. Sarah had attached herself leech-like to his upper body and he was bashing her off the door frame as he tried to swing free. I wasn't surprised that the plumbers never showed. The second time I rang them after dropping Sarah and Adam to school. I made sure to have Handel playing and I hinted that I was in the process of whipping up Nigella's Chocolate Cloud Cake, should they by any chance be able to drop by that afternoon.

'We'll be there,' said Anto, 'never fear.'

Two o' clock came and went. I spent ages gliding down the hallway past the phone, watching it peripherally, so that it wouldn't know I wanted it to ring, and then not ring on purpose. Finally I gave up, lifted the handset and dialled the number on those lovely soft pad keys. Anto answered.

'Sorry love, got a bit of a job on in Rathdrum, I'll be up to you tomorrow around three.'

Anto and his sidekick Kevin arrived at five to six. Sarah and Adam were threading spaghetti hoops onto their fingers and flicking them at each other. They stopped briefly for Sarah to say in the megaphone voice allotted to the under-fives;

'Mammy, that man is fat, and that one,' she paused to make a sweeping motion across her tummy – 'is flat.'

My ruddy faced embarrassment as I contemplated Kevin's uncannily steamrollered appearance, matched the hearty complexion of the horizontally challenged Anto.

'Let's have a look then,' was all Anto said.

I pointed them in the direction of the bathroom.

'It's the shower,' said Anto when they came downstairs. 'The waste or the seal. We'll have to have another look to be sure.'

Kevin said nothing, he stayed behind Anto, shuttling from

side to side like a skeptical crab, cracking his nicotine-stained fingers and pushing back long strands of lanky hair.

'We'll be over first thing tomorrow,' Anto announced magnanimously with an extravagant gesture of the hand.

I felt a sudden surge of elation. I had been put at the top of the list.

The next morning, as the clock edged past the agreed time, I sat watching the brown stain spread its pleated frills ever outward. It morphed like a Rorschach inkblot test into representations of butterflies and bat-faced old geezers. The plumbers turned up just as the stain acquired a leering gummy-toothed smile. To be fair to them, they wasted no time and headed upstairs immediately; Anto heaving and rumbling as he went, sending ominous vibrations through the floor joists, Kevin pitter pattering in his wake like a tiny cat. After a while I filled the kettle to the comforting sounds of industrious clatter and banging, the odd mellifluous whistle. I put on the radio but their talk of bad weather and threatened flooding made me uneasy.

'Cloud cake,' I shouted up the stairs.

'Beautiful,' said Anto as he licked the third slice of cake off the stubby ends of his calloused fingers. 'There is no love sincerer than the love of food, says Shaw,' he told me.

Kevin had gone out for a smoke. Anto rubbed his hands together to loosen the crumbs that had lodged in the chiselled cracks of his palms.

'Looks like it's the waste,' he said. 'We've opened everything up, taken out the shower tray. We'll be back tomorrow with the parts.'

'Oh,' I said, backing away from the door through which he was evidently preparing to leave.

The next day I placed myself on the sofa which had a view of the front driveway as well as the television. While I waited, I watched repeats of *Property Ladder* and *About the House*.

Between you and me, I had recently begun to fancy myself as a property developer, although now with the credit crunch and tumbling house prices, I was starting to rethink. 'You must have the confidence to deal effectively with your tradesmen, in order to bring the project in on schedule,' the presenter was saying. Above my head the ceiling was beginning to bubble and froth. One section resembled an upside-down Baked Alaska, hanging decoratively to the left of the chandelier. I had to take a firm line with Anto. I put my hair in an assertive pony-tail and rang his number.

The phone was answered.

'Anto,' I gasped.

'It's Kevin,' came the monotone from the other end.

I realised I had never heard Kevin speak before. There was a sort of Vincent Price quality to his delivery.

'He can't come,' he said in response to my question.

'It's his uncle.'

'Oh?' I said.

'He's dead,' said Kevin.

'Oh, well, I'm so ...' I offered.

'He's at the funeral. He'll be with you,' there was a pause as he became audibly distant, his voice replaced by crackles and scratches 'on Thursday.'

I met Sandra Brennan at the school gate. Her husband had just finished converting their garage to a playroom with materials he'd sourced from recycling and exchange websites. I told her about my problems with the plumbers, finishing with the sad news about the plumber's uncle. For a moment I thought she'd swallowed a peanut. She threw her head back and her eyes began to water. Her throat emitted a kind of whooping hack. I had just come round behind her and braced myself for the Heimlich manoeuvre when she waved me away while drawing in quick wheezy breaths. It was only then I realised she was laughing.

'Dead!' she chortled. 'Gone to a funeral!'

Luckily Adam's class came out into their line and I made my escape. Sandra's very nice but people have been saying that perhaps baby number five was one surprise too many.

On Thursday I eschewed lattes in the new arts centre café with the girls in order to wait for Anto and Kevin. By now I had cordoned off the area under the bulging ceiling with my two-year-old Italian leather sofa. Denis was due back at the weekend and wasn't pleased to hear that the job wasn't completed. He informed me that the project deliverable was well overdue. I switched on the computer hoping that technology could help tackle the delay. I tracked variables and estimated timelines. Then I gave up and Googled plumbers, toying with the treacherous idea of Getting Someone Else In halfway through the job. I found a plumber whose website blurb made touching promises to value my time, return my calls, even to communicate gently and considerately on site. Moisture began to seep through my vented eye sockets. It was the plumber-client relationship I had dreamed of, but never had.

My heart thudded and juddered like an air locked pipe as I rang Anto's number. This time it was Anto himself who answered.

'You're not here,' I said.

'Come again?' said Anto.

'You promised to be with me first thing.'

I couldn't suppress my resentment at being relegated.

'You're obviously with someone else. You could've told me,' I wailed.

'It's my uncle. He kicked the bucket.'

'The bucket?' I glanced up at the sagging ceiling and all at once realised I should've put a bucket under the melting Baked Alaska. I gathered my thoughts.

'But the funeral was last week,' I blurted, a tad insensitively.

'What's that?' he asked.

'Kevin told me.'

'Ah yes, right,' he said, then followed a sliver of a pause, 'That was my maternal uncle, this uncle is on my father's side. He's being buried this morning up in Sugarloaf Cemetery.'

How I wished then that the floor would open up and swallow me but preferably not the upstairs bathroom floor which in all probability might.

I hung up the phone and contemplated the situation in almost exquisite silence, punctuated only by the drip, drip of the hidden leak. Even now, I cannot tell you if I made my decision out of solidarity or suspicion. I tugged a long dark woolen coat out of the wardrobe and prepared to leave. As I closed the front door after me, I thought I heard the rumble and growl of falling plaster.

It was a frosty morning, the dew evaporating in the early morning sun. As I approached the cemetery I could see the mourners congregating, the steam from their breaths swirling into the air like a newly installed sauna. There, outside the gates, a fleet of Ford Transits in shades of Used to be White and Almost Emergency Red were parked, reverse parked and double parked all the way down the road and into the distance; Bathroom Installers, Drain Management, Plugs and Pipes, every conceivable plumbing service known to man and sometimes to women. They were gathered in their masses, respectfully attired in their buttoned-up overcoats and shiny leather shoes, heads bent, their tears so genuine and profuse that leaking taps didn't have a patch on them.

After the service there were refreshments in Kennedy's on the Kilruddery Road. They sat, this brotherhood of plumbers, sipping their pints of tea, and biting into thick sandwiches made with proper ham cut off the bone. I found Anto with a newspaper and a mouth full of sausage roll. I shook his hand.

'*Because I could not stop for death. It kindly stopped for me,*' he said mournfully.

I found the talk of stopping too much to bear. Facing into the

73

devastation at home, I knew that I was leaving behind those who mattered most. As I stepped away, Anto flicked open his newspaper.

'That was a good one, that'll take some beating,' he remarked to a fellow mourner. Scanning the obituaries, he sighed and pondered 'Which one to next?'

Pushing open the door, I stepped outside where it was now chucking it down and floods were forecast.

Last Tango with Dinosaurs

It was awkward about the dinosaurs. No-one knew what to do with the Brontosaurus in the park. On Wednesday a child digging to China on the beach found dinosaur eggs, still warm. On Friday a Pleisosaurus was spotted lunging at the hydrofoil in Ryde. By the following week, the Pterodactyls had killed some seagulls at Shanklin.

And now the tea dancing was cancelled ... A plant-eater had jeopardized the floral arrangements at the local hall and all activities were suspended, including the Senior Tango competition.

'*Polacanthas* it says here,' Reggie pointed at the front page of the evening edition.

Ivy peered over his shoulder.

'Agapanthas,' *I* thought.' Ivy put three sugars in Reggie's tea and handed it to him. 'Whatever it's called, it's spoiling our fun.'

At first people thought it was a nuisance. Two Beryls on a bus tour dropped their ice creams when a Ventnor velociraptor nipped their ankles. On Sunday, a family felt the dinosaurs at the amusement park in Sandown were 'too realistic.'

The junior news reporters at the *Island Chronicle* were also troubled. 'How do you spell T-rex the long way?' Stewart wanted to know.

'T Y Ranno,' Jenny said. 'And saw with a 'u' ...But I didn't think they'd spotted any yet?'

Stewart tapped his pencil against his teeth. 'You never know your luck ...'

Dinosaurs – or more usually their bones – had always been an Isle of Wight tourist attraction. Now crowds flocked to the island to see the beasts there for real. Hotels and B&Bs booked up. The Jurassic bonanza was such that the council turned a blind eye when a Hypsilophodon stripped the Botanic Gardens and when an Iguanadon squashed a man hedge-trimming in Newport. An information pamphlet was issued, suggesting that visitors view the creatures from the safety of their cars. It also explained how to tell carnivores from herbivores, while pointing out that short sighted herbivores might not be able to tell the difference between a toddler and a leaf.

There began to be murmurs of dissent when a Neoventor ate a family at Cowes, but they weren't really anyone important.

'So it says right here,' said Reggie behind his newspaper again.

'Everyone's important to someone,' Ivy tutted as she fed her beloved poodles Paddles and Piddles. These were the last of a long line of prize winners she'd shown at Crufts. Her dog handling had been famed before she retired to the island.

In mid-summer news came in that the bones of two walkers had been found. An Eotyrannus was blamed. In light of the 'regrettable deaths' it was proposed to cordon off an area to the south as a Jurassic Park.

'Haven't they watched the movie?' Jenny sighed as she typed the lead story headline: *Tenders requested for perimeter fencing.*

When a busload of town councilors on a junket was consumed by some Velociraptors an emergency meeting of the remaining council members was called and the funding for the park was pushed through.

Soon after the fencing went up, Ivy was out walking Paddles and Piddles when she noticed that there were now even more dinosaurs prowling the coast. On close inspection it seemed that the perimeter fences had been altered in such a way that now island residents were contained *within* the Jurassic Park and the dinosaurs roamed free on the outside.

When September came, college students couldn't return to university as the ports were blocked. Tourism faltered, since the only method of reaching B&Bs was a stealth trek through pterodactyl territory. Food could no longer be imported from the mainland. Hydrofoils and cargo ships were chomped, train tracks torn from the ground. To top it all off a woman from the Needles missed her sister's wedding in Southampton.

Jurassic Fiasco! Drastic action should be taken, read Reggie as the street outside shook. Ivy peered around the net curtain. The T-rex had arrived, triumphant and sassy like a Rasta gang leader. The creature was flattening numbers 10 to 21 with a flick of his tail. Reggie's prizewinning allotment had recently been demolished by a careless triceratops. It didn't seem fair. She tutted. Reggie put down his newspaper and reached out for her.

Ivy let herself be pulled down on his lap. Reggie nuzzled her powdery old neck. Within their embrace the newspaper with its pictures of coastal devastation rustled.

'I don't know, Ivy ...' Reggie sighed, 'we will fight them on the beaches ... but where's the army now, the navy, the helicopters?'

They were interrupted by an ominous yelp. Through the window they saw that Piddles had become nibbles for the formidable T-Rex. Ivy fell against Reggie's chest in despair.

That night Ivy couldn't sleep. She sat downstairs and sipped tea at the Formica table. Dinosaur roars rebounded from the coast. The old lady fretted. Many families had been forced to evacuate inland. The Meals on Wheels had gone into overdrive. Piddles was dead and Reggie's courgettes had exploded under rogue dinosaur feet. What could be done? Ivy patted the sleepy head of her remaining, obedient poodle. She stared, then stood up suddenly, full of vigour.

Next morning Ivy trotted with her walking stick down the half-flattened street. She took a bus as close to the coast as it would take her. The sun's dawn rays spread over the countryside like the soft, sparkly sponge fingers you put in a trifle. She slowly hobbled the last mile to the perimeter fence, hoping that Reggie would find the note she'd left on the Teasmaid.

At the fence she found a lumbering triceratops, with no sign of the usual Velociraptors. She didn't like to think what *they* might be doing elsewhere. Ivy had her gripes with politicians but she'd found herself very upset about the coach load of town councilors. There'd been no need for that kind of thing.

The note to Reggie had been a lie. *Gone to Margie's to help with Meals on Wheels.* She hated deceiving Reggie but she couldn't just stand by, desperate times called for well ... courage. Ivy's mother Ethel had been in the ambulances in WW2. She didn't just stop and fold her arms did she? She didn't just take videos with her I-phone from her bedroom window and put them on YouTube like the young people were doing. Tony from the Community Education Centre had explained that one chap had got 5 million hits. Ivy didn't approve of hitting in the slightest.

Now Ivy looked right into the eye of the triceratops. In her firmest voice she said 'Sit'. The triceratops began growling. *'Drastic action,'* the newspaper had said. Ivy slipped her stick through a small opening in the fence. She might not approve of hitting but needs must. She gave the dinosaur a tiny tap on the rump to make him pay attention. Barbara Woodhouse would have approved. Ivy wondered momentarily whether Barbara's dog training videos from the eighties were on that YouTube thingy.

Now, just as Ivy had trained her wonderful but now deceased poodle Piddles, she went through a number of steps to take command of the wayward dinosaur. Piddles had been a handful to begin with but with consistency of voice and intent, she'd got the better of his foibles – even the piddling. Now she seemed to be having some success with this triceratops and the others that soon arrived. They seemed to respond to her voice's light ring of approval and the dog biscuits she tossed over the fence. *They've probably had enough of all that wanton chaos* Ivy wagered.

At about eleven Ivy was in need of sustenance. The café on Ryde promenade that served cream teas was now out of bounds and all her dog biscuits were gone. Ivy felt quite cross. She made her way wearily back to the bus stop and hoped that the driver hadn't been eaten in the meantime.

When Ivy arrived home Reggie was watering the hanging baskets. The residents committee was picking up bricks from flattened homes. Boys and girls were playing hide and seek among the tottering walls like children after the Blitz. Young Stewart from the newspaper was watching footage of the T-Rex from someone's phone. As Ivy watched the valiant efforts of the folk around her Reggie nipped inside. He returned with a cup of tea and some Bourbon Creams. 'My love,' he said. She knew he knew she was up to something

Day after day she went to the perimeter leaving the same note for Reggie, even after Meals on Wheels Margie got eaten by a plesiosaurus while attempting a shopping trip to the mainland. Ivy's dinosaur training efforts began to pay off. The dinosaurs became more placid. The daily death toll plummeted significantly to single digits which made it easier for newspaper lad Stewart to tot up. He reported that because of Ivy the dinosaurs now played catch and generally sat when commanded instead of snapping the residents into their jaws. He was too young to have heard of Barbara Woodhouse so he called Ivy "Supernanny for Dinos." Jenny did a *day in the life* piece with photographs of Ivy and Reggie in 'happier times' clutching rosettes for their poodles and courgettes.

Soon Ivy was bestowed *in abstensia* with an order of chivalry from the Queen but Dame Ivy's work was far from done. She'd conquered the Triceretops, Polacanthas and the rest of the herbivores but the Velociraptors – flighty and crazed like spaniels – were still tricky. The T-Rex resembled the worst kind of rescue dog, damaged and dangerously unpredictable even for the most accomplished trainer.

For his part, Reggie was concerned about Ivy. She was worn out, poor love. Despite her success, dinosaurs still roamed in numbers and continued to wreak devastation if only by inadvertently treading on things when fetching thrown balls. When a triceratops accidentally nipped the head off Ivy's remaining poodle Paddles he felt it was time for action. Who knew but it might be Ivy's head next.

Reggie had a think. The dinosaurs had seemed to come from no-where. But he had a hunch about their true origin.

Down near the coast was an old tunnel, used in the early 1900s for a now discarded rail line. It was said that this tunnel connected underground with caves that led right into the heart of the island. Reggie, island born and bred, knew the caves were spacious and deep and had been mentioned specifically in ancient stories of the 'dragon island.'

Next day at the perimeter fence Ivy felt a tap on the shoulder. She turned, surprised, embracing Reggie. He whispered into her ear, outlining the strategy.

He touched her face gently. 'Do you think you can do it?'

Ivy nodded. Reggie reached over and cut the fence wire with his garden pliers.

'Walkies!' commanded Ivy. Reggie clicked his tongue. Together they led the parade of bellowing, lumbering beasts along the coastal track until they arrived at the tunnel.

'Now what?' Ivy wondered.

'Senior Tango, my dear.' Reggie reached for his wife. They clasped each other then moved as one towards the tunnel opening.

Close to the entrance Ivy tapped her stick again. "Walk on!" She commanded. A doe-eyed diplodocus took the lead, the huge length of him lunging with primal instinct towards the tunnel opening. Ivy and Reggie watched the dinosaurs follow in unison, like a flock at a sheep dog trials. Into the darkness the beasts went. The T-Rex was last, his huge bulk loosening stones as he pushed through, causing a final landslide that sealed the tunnel entrance. There was momentary silence then Ivy and Reggie emerged, humming, from the dust.

Tourists still came. Rumour morphed to hearsay, then to legend, then myth. When the clamour of each day subsided, a rumbling sound could be heard – thunder, maybe, or a tea dance rumba, the unending roar of the sea, or the sound of ancient beasts now safe in the belly of the island.

All that Thinking

Before I was born, I danced in my mother's womb. I pressed against the inside with my flexing feet. I dreamed of the beginning that was the past, I imagined the beginning yet to come. I was attached to my new life with a coil that would in time be severed. And when I knew the time would come to break through the skin into the next world, I said goodbye. I cried where no crying could be heard.

When I arrived here and grew, I loved my mother with the devotion of a small puppy. I pressed myself against her legs and suffocated in her skirts. She was kind, homely and distracted. She made scones in the morning and went to stare at rainbows with flour on her hands. She moved through the house like the ephemeral hint of spring that fades after days. She put the dinner on the table, she brushed lint from my father's shoulder with the disappearing quality of an exhaled breath. The more he called with menacing impatience 'Where are you?' fastening her to the iron of his will, the more she seemed to recede into the fractal chaos of the paisley wallpaper. Many years later she slipped out of life in a November fog, tracing my skin as she passed. Now she roams out there at the side of the hill, skids across the sky on cumulus.

Between then and now I loved a boy and he loved me. He was an ordinary thing, a sort of squat being, like a standing stone with his face carved in with spirals, a smattering of sunlit lichen for his hair. But the taste of him was like cold water from a bubbling stream and the feel of him was swathes of yellow silk, stone in the hot summer.

I am thinking of his skin. The way it sprung back against my young fingertips. I read once about a woman who had no fingerprints. And now when I press against him, I no longer make a mark because where he is I am not. He has passed by osmosis to the other side of the universe's skin.

I am a spirit, not free, not spirited. I slip through gaps in understanding, between the said and the interpreted. Between memory and recollection. But I know this isn't how you want to know me. You want to recognise me by the colour of my coat, by the height and the shape of me, by the peg you can put me on, the box you can label.

I am a dedicated mother, I am a wife, I am a respectable citizen, I vote in elections and if I don't it's because I can't get a babysitter. I am a church goer. I go there and I sit and I look up and I wait. For grace. For that feeling like balsam on the chest, the clear-headedness, the relieved alveoli.

Where I live is a bowl, a hole in the earth, a smallholding dug out of the bog. I am a hobbit with my hobbit children. I live with a man my father chose for me. An old man. Every morning I gather up the peelings of his dead skin, the gnarled roots from his toes, I give him back his teeth and light a fire to send a glimmer of warmth into his crumbling bones. He is, through the unlikely triumph of dying salmon, the flesh father of these children. But while the old man pushed down upon me the boy was in my head, streaking through the cortical folds, embedded in the cells, like a pebble sucked into the sand. I held my breath then with the old man straining for legacy. I did not want to breathe in that life. But when it was over and the old man returned to sleep I got up and watched the reluctant dawn slink around the lintels. I remembered that my man boy was still out there somewhere and then the sun nudged over the hill and poured its honey.

'I love you,' I whisper later into the stale sheets as I tear them from the bed. 'I did love you, will love you, used to love you, will have loved you, have been loving you in the past perfect, the present continuous, the simple future, the simple past, the future perfect continuous, the simple present, the present

83

perfect.'

If it has skin, does the universe have ears?

The old man has me do the farm accounts. He says 'them bloody computers are beyond me'. He says it with a righteous pride, because he is rooted by his wellington boots to the natural, to earthy manure threaded with straw, to the heady silage, the chicken shit and the fecund coop. And he breathes in first hand air that comes over the fields that have his name on and he is a god, the god of smallholdings.

I make things add up. I create columns down which the money pours and make rows of neatly planted investments. It's not as bad as you might think, a farm of land here, another there, a harvestable peat bog, a quota of milkers, a herd of good looking yearlings, plenty hens, spare eggs and a flock of daubed sheep strolling the mountain. My father is, as they say around here 'no fool' and he bartered me for a man with a plethora of money stuffed under the mattress. I married him on a spring morning, the last Saturday before Lent. And the man boy disappeared.

Where did he go? He was here once, between my fists, flesh and fabric. And now he has dissolved into the universe. There are no stories of him, no tales that have a life beyond their maker.

The old man climbs the slow stairs to bed. But with the speed and deftness he uses when clipping the chain to the milking cows neck I clip a wire we usually use for the phone to the back of the computer. Then I wait for this ambling retrograde version of progress, the slow train to the hub and connection.

More than a hundred years ago men braved roaring seas in ships to set a cable on the ocean bed between Valentia, a stone's throw from here, across the Atlantic to a place called Hearts Content in Newfoundland. And so sometimes when it is night and the old man's sleeping cells futilely attempt regeneration, I surf across the wide divide, cast my nets, scour for evidence to find you newly.

The computer screen is a lit portal. I click and shuttle. I traverse the cyberverse in an instant, coming face to face with the man boy's laugh, the wide mouth and the tumbling lava. I press my mouth against his in the darkness, in the bright searing light, in the sun's blast, in the nuclear winter, in the dark side of the moon, in the tangle of cables, arachnoids web, sticky filaments. I am here, I am there, cut adrift in zero gravity in inky outer space where time expands relentlessly or I am skulking in the murk of memory, ghettos of forgetfulness, kicking at newspaper ghosts.

In the morning I brush away cobwebs, I braid the children's hair before releasing them into the outside. There they tumble into the hollow and make fairytale castles out of great rocks heaved into the valley by ancient glacial ice. The girls, of which there are two, tramp around sedge tufted hummocks becoming knights and princesses by turn, slipping in and out of skins, forging and swapping identities. They ride ghost horses through the heather. They are as blonde as Nordic icemen, as blonde as their father and I are not.

I have one more child, a toddler-baby boy who I steer out the kitchen door into the morning by his compact bottom. I recognise in him a concentrated expression, an intensity between the eyebrows. *You.* I think. But perhaps the expression was first mine, until I came across the mirror of you, uttered that euphoric primordial Yes! Knew you. Knew.

When I look out I see the terraced hills, stacked on each other. The approached crests laugh with duplicity, for beyond each achieved pinnacle is another one, spinning another tale of the wondrous summit. So I live in an inverted pyramid incubating my dreams like the Egyptians, waiting for homeless spirits to carry portentous messages between us while we sleep. And I wake in the morning with the sea that was once in this valley on my pillow and the shape of your footprints on the shore filling up and flattening.

But there is a thin skin between this space-time universe and the one beside it. And sometimes I wonder if I can tear a hole in it with all this thinking. Like when the children pick at a loose stitch in a jumper and keep on worrying it until it rips. There was a particular day when the old man had gone to the mart with two Charley yearlings, flippity gibbets of things, flailing with good humour, kicking up their heels with the fallacy of freedom. All day the doors of the rooms I was in were rattling and banging as if someone was trying to get in. And the trees shook with an impatient frenzy and the sky closed and lent back in turns like folding and unfolding paper.

I have a feeling that it is when this universe seems most solid that things can press through it: memories, glimpses, photographs, letters.

And one of these mornings I watch the postman's van come round the side of the hill. There is nothing to see yet but I keep it in sight, watch it creeping up the laneway of the house on the opposing hill, see the tyres nipped by lunatic dogs, hear, even from this distance the crunch and splutter of gravel under the wheels. And I know there will be a letter and it will be from the man boy and when I open it he will come pouring out, the sense and the smell and the evidence of him and I will press the letter against my face, inhale the cells.

You'll ask me why, won't you? Why I didn't say no when my father made me the price of his vanity. Why I didn't fashion a flying device from old sticks and animal hide and glide away from the top of the mountain out of his mean reach. You want me to do something. To follow my heart. And take action. But a cliché is a blunt instrument, it cannot tear a hole big enough to see through. You will wonder why I don't magnetize the fierce coil that spins within and follow the pull, step out of the door and catch the hands of my happy-go-lucky hobbits and run in your direction.

In the evenings I twist the papers into flammable bows and set them into the grate. The old man nods as I crouch and grunt among the hearth's ashes. This is as it is and all is right with him.

He has had his supper and his belly is lined with the fat of other animals. He talks of the price of cattle and he knows how to skin the turf bog and slice it in pieces that begin as moist as slugs and dry out through the summer like crackling leaves. I nod back at him but the slick film that gathers on the mug of cold tea by his elbow separates us. I get up, I pace, I look out of the window, I run my fingers over the cold keyboard of the computer, riding over the bumps like a car on this country track, rattling and shaking, shuttling back to the main road. The old man nods again but it is the nod of sleep, the little death that precedes the one that awaits him. The old man dozes by the warm fire, feels the heat, the lull, the body comfort. He dreams of the womb.

You will ask me. But I sit down and wait. I take up some knitting and the fire spits. Embers scorch the rug, blazing, then collapsing into black holes. I knit to the end of a row, I turn the whole thing round and knit back the other way. I add row upon row and the rows are the generations building on one another – human history – the current and the previous, ancestors disappearing further and further down into the fabric. My fingers fly. I drop a stitch. I go back and retrieve it or maybe not. If I don't go back I leave the universe unravelling. The old man snorts in his sleep. I put down my knitting and take away the cold tea.

Outside there are a billion stars and the moon rises whole and yellow over the hill. Nothing is moving. I long for the moon but I do not go out. I look at it through the glass, resting my hand on the pane. I wait all these nights as the old man edges to the end of the row where I can slip him off my needle. Breath running out. Because death, like birth, tears a hole that a whole person can get through. Then I will slip through the gap in the wall into the passageway that runs between these dimensions. I will tear down the cobwebs. I will sweep my laughter down all the long corridors and find you.

Letter

You pick me up in the morning from the mat on the floor under the letter box, or perhaps from the hall table, amidst a pile of unopened mail from recipients long gone, no forwarding address, forgotten, perhaps even deceased.

You run your finger along the tight edge of me. I am long, slim, pale, like a ghost from the old days. I may seem empty, even though I am not. I am etched with your name. And your location; the device by which I have been brought to you, into your long hand, the kink in the bone of your ring finger.

You look at me. You're eyes are not quite what they once were, you pull me close, push me back again, the focus adjusting. You see the way the letters of you are formed on my outside, the curl of them; the places where I leave you trailing and where you are indented.

You think of bringing me close to your face, of breathing me in, perhaps even vaguely touching your lips to my starched skin, but you are in the hallway and there are voices from the other flats, perhaps from the stairs, footsteps approaching. Because you are about to go out you don't go back and leave me on your kitchen table with the maple effect veneer and the dark mug stain and the microscopic grains of cereal your single diligence missed. I do not have to wait there; while the isosceles of sun slides across me through the mid-morning leaving me basking and warm; while the afternoon comes to the hum of the ancient fridge freezer the landlord will not change; to the evening and the lonely dusk and the sound of cars splishing lamplit puddles against the kerb. If you left me there, you would see me firstly when you walked into the empty flat – as you turned on the light – you would see me alone, on the kitchen table, the herald of your longing. You would pounce on me, tear me open, feed on my words, so hungry and weary. You would put me down temporarily sated, you would put your head on the table and sleep, your cheek against me.

You are on your way out, late, for all you have to do, for all you have to accomplish so that you can pay your bills, your due, so you can construct a life of brick and mortar, sticks and straw, so that you can go to the supermarket and not think about it so precisely.

You put me into your inside jacket pocket, against the rise and fall of your breathing, against the thud of your heart. I hear keys jingle, the door slam, feel the descent of steps, the propulsion of hurry, the vibration of the van, the lift of your arm as you turn the steering wheel. I am flat against you, reviving from the energy that circulates your body, grudgingly, when the weather is cold, the demisters are playing up and the traffic is heavy and when you drive home in the falling evening as tight as a fist crushing paper, tight from the trials of politeness and toil, finicky customers, second-rate exchanges, ham sandwiches and lukewarm tea in noisy laybys. But you are warm now, in the morning, when the residue of sleep still soothes you like a mother's hand, soft on the brow, when the engine turns over first time and the sky is the sea seen from a Greek island, the clouds, white stone houses stood against it.

Your first job is nearby. You park. Get out. A door opens. You go in. I hear your voice, – deeper, more robust, than I had remembered it, speaking to a potential customer. You are quoting her for some shelves and a new door for the downstairs utility. At some point she laughs. I don't know why – I cannot hear what you have said – but there is flirtation in her laugh, in the bubble of it, in the duration. I hear that from inside your pocket, against you. But you leave her, knowing perhaps that she will call you back, engage you, for something more than your knowledge of angle brackets and dovetailed joints. I feel the lightness in the way you move, hear you whistle like someone's Dad. You close the door of the van firmly, with a little optimism.

The engine roars into life.

You drive along the coast road – I smell brine, hear seagulls screech with greed. You make another call, an older lady who addresses you with clipped gentility. I can tell from the slow strong beat of your heart that she somehow makes you fond. It is hardly from the encounter itself but from some remembrance engendered, some archetypal granny of boiled sweets and powdery skin.

At lunchtime you stop the van at a place high up with a view of everything. You roll down the window and open a bottle that fizzes. You eat the sandwiches. They are cheese this time and you remembered the pickle.

You slide your hand into your pocket. You take me out. You hold me with the tips of your fingers. You trace your hand over the length of me. You rest me on your legs while you take another drink. You put me on the passenger seat. You look out where you can see sea, boats, sand, land, birds suspended in the air, a low wall, grass tufts shaking in the wind. You look at me. You look.

You pick me up. You want to open me. You stare through my skin now, restless for faint traces of what's inside. But my skin is not thin; I do not reveal anything except the co-ordinates of you. You want to know, but you want to wait because there will never be another moment of not knowing, because everything that is sweet is in the bud and everything that is open starts to turn.

After lunch it is hot. We travel south-west so that the sun blasts into the car. You take off your jacket into which you returned me. When you go into the next place you leave the jacket in the car. So I wait, absorbing the smell of you, inert, but singing on the inside. I wait, thinking about you, about you before, about how I find you now and all the layers in between, the shifting that goes on throughout a lifetime, the changing nuance between the first letter and the last. And when all that thinking is done I listen to the sound of sirens, distant, and laughter passing close by in the street.

When you come back you are distracted, coiled. The sand slips quicker at the end of day and you cannot stop it. You check your phone, listening to the backed-up messages, you leaf through your work order book, you tut, you force on the engine, it stutters. You push out into the traffic, revving. Someone blasts the horn. You swear. The rain begins, coming in staccato splatters. You have put your jacket back on. I snooze in the white noise of water between rubber and tarmac, frantic wipers.

When I wake we are moving. You are climbing out of the van, locking it. After a day of languor, the momentum is thrilling. I lift, lift, lift in your pocket up the step, step, step. You click open the door, washing away a sea of junk mail, unregarded. What if I was ....? There are more steps, dizzy ascending. We pause at your door, more keys. Teatime sounds come from the other flats. Clanks, sizzles, voices turned up and then off. You take me in.

Inside, you take off your jacket. Your steps cross the room, fade, return. You slide your hands inside the jacket pocket, your fingers find me. You slide me out. In the corridor there is a door opening then closing. Hot onions cooking.

You lean me up against a jar on the worktop, olive oil with a gnarled chilli inside it. I can see the toaster, the draining board with a long glass upturned, a crusty loaf, sliced open, the knife prostrate beside it, the little indented curves in its sharp edge.

You make chops for your dinner. Lamb. You sprinkle a little rosemary and mint on them under the grill. You have it with the bread, and a thin gravy you make in the pan at the end. I look at you but not as much as you might imagine. I focus on the part of your face at the top of the cheekbone, the soft place where you are still twenty, the curve of your lip where it disappears. I glance from time to time at you as you eat; your satisfaction in meat tender with gravy, the resistance of bread. You have the radio on now, something quiet, where the announcer unfurls her words in devoted tones and the music is something that you can sink into. You sit, still at the table. Your legs loosen and your fingers unbud like a baby's sleep surrender. So you sit in the womb of the stopped moment, folded in. I am here on the counter top. I love you. You look up.

You stand, a stretch lengthening your chest, your arm flailing forward, your shoulder settling. You pick up your plate and bring it to the counter. You put it down at the edge of the draining board. You pick me up and hold me. You take me to the sofa, sit down with me. The woman on the radio murmurs sleepily.

You open me. My skin tears a little. You take what is inside out. I am unfolded, seen. You touch me. Unconsciously, leaning the tip of your finger against my side you read my words. They go in, through your eyes; ink, receptor, synapse, heart. Sometimes you peer closer, I am not always legible. Sometimes you want to be sure of what you're seeing; sometimes you do not quite understand me, although you want to. And what do I do? Do I creep into the chambers of you, phosphorescent caves, memories calcified and dripping? Do I press the shape of me into the cells of you or do I glide through and out like a breath of jasmine. Do I? Do ...

When you read me. That is the moment I am real. I am held steady within co-ordinates. I move. I resonate. I walk, breathe, talk. Here I am and my voice comes from the inside in your head, leaving through your ears. You can no longer hear the arguments from the flat across the way, the woman with the dyed blonde hair complaining about how he never really listens to her anymore, about how they talk about the dishes now and the bills – not anymore about how she makes him horny when she puts on her lipstick in the morning, or how she loves the back of his neck and the sound of him singing to Sinatra in the shower. So many things not said anymore.

I shiver in your hands. And as your eyes move down, I am falling, draining away and you drink me in. You turn me over. You take in the last of me. You smile. Now that you have read me, you are more certain and I more vulnerable. You stop smiling. You fold me in. You hesitate, looking at me peripherally before pushing me back into the envelope. You stop. You hold me for a split second just where I can hear your heart. Thump.

You put me away. You have a place for me. You slide me into the cardboard box the radio was bought in. You hum to yourself, you wash up. Later you go to bed.

Unwritten

'I love you,' said the man at the book signing.

He was one of the last. The shop was closing. The staff were starting to turn off the lights. She was sitting in the glow of a table lamp with her latest novel in stacks around her. There had been a respectable turn out, her nerves had faded once she'd seen a queue of several.

'I've read all your books,' he said. 'I feel I know you.'

'That's nice,' she said. 'Who will I write it for?'

'For me,' he said. 'For Tom.'

He loved her. He must mean her work. 'I just love you, you're brilliant,' they'd gushed earlier.

He stood aside momentarily. He let the last two ladies with their plastic shopping bags hand over their books and ask for a personalised message.

She was distracted; she had to ask them twice what she should write. She was aware of the man at her shoulder, his presence in the dark, rubbing out the edges of her on that side, melding her with his shadow.

She wasn't afraid. She stood up to get her things, the back of her neck felt vulnerable, virginal but the air was still warm from the press of people. The sensation she felt was from the inside, not from air.

He came forward, lit up. 'The things you say,' he said. 'I know what you mean.'

'It's fiction,' she said, looking at her bag as she rummaged for her keys.

'Never do anything to alienate your readers,' her publisher had told her. 'Be courteous, friendly and uncontroversial – try and hide your frown lines.'

'It's fict ...' she repeated, more softly, looking at him. But she saw in his eyes. He knew. She had always been better at atmosphere than plot but she thought it had been enough to distract them; the narrative was the shiny neon light guiding them to the playhouse. They weren't meant to look too closely at the subtext, duck into the alleyway or the authentic cookhouse on route, or some red light backstage dressing room where she sat half-undressed in front of a mirror, all shallow breath and heaving breasts, rouge, heart on sleeve. I solemnly decline to let you read between the lines.

She thought he would kiss her, he came so close but he closed the book and made for the door. She chatted with the bookshop manager, thanked everyone and stepped into the street, black, damp, quiet.

Her car was parked just down the now empty city centre thoroughfare. As she walked, water, under the tyres of a moving vehicle, whished like shorebound waves.

He was sitting in the café window. She recognised the shape of him without truly seeing. The glare from the café flared in her face, like a blush. There was the quickening of her footbeat heartbeat footbeat. The light subsided, dropped. There was a gap between the buildings, all dark, wet on the inside, up the walls. The next building was shut up, gloomy. She saw her car alone on the street.

He was not the only one in the café. There was a couple holding hands, tightly, in anticipation of separation. The owner was staring into space. He had a moustache and a head of black, oily hair, flat on top. He looked like he'd just slid out from under a car. He was sweating, wiping his hands with a cloth. He wasn't staring into space. He was looking at his own reflection in the café window, against the night. He was seeing what he had come to after all these years. He didn't sigh.

She sat down across from *him*. Behind his head were plumes of smoke. A heavily jowled woman puffed and coughed in the corner. She had a chin mole. She was out of a fairytale. She was eating the gingerbread. She rummaged in a canvas bag and took out an apple, green on one side, red on the other. She plonked it on the table and continued to rummage. She looked at the owner. His lip quivered slightly.

The author looked at Tom. She wasn't sure of the name yet. The oil cloth was greasy but someone had put forget-me-nots in glass vases on each of the tables. He began to tell her how he had come across her books, which one he had liked best, but in the end she took his hand and they held on tight, in anticipation of separation. After a while they went out, he kept holding her hand up the steps to his flat.

He wanted to meet her, tomorrow, again and again. He said they had so much in common, so much to talk about. He said this while he traced a line from her fingertips, along her arm, across her shoulder and neck, up to her cheek over which he laid his warm palm. She rolled against him with familiarity. They lay along the length of each other, restful, as if they had always done. But they didn't talk then. They played music instead which they made love to, then didn't, just listened, the notes playing in and around their heads, all joy, and then he kissed her and it all began again.

Later his eyes tired from the fill of her and his eyelashes dipped.

She slipped from the bed while he dreamed of them walking in parks, watching movies, buying mince.

She was naked but warm and she saw the bookcases and CD racks with the books, not only hers but other authors she loved, music she was into. She looked into his wardrobe where he hung his clothes with the same sort of absentmindedness as her own. She took out a shirt and breathed him in, as if he was dead, as if she was saying goodbye.

She got dressed and went into the kitchen. There were two cups where they'd had tea and bourbon biscuits. They were facing each other on the otherwise empty table, just the tiniest residue of crumbs spilled during laughter.

Before she left she went to look at him, searing him into her memory. She already felt nostalgia, the first sharp flickers of pain. She felt in her pocket for her notebook and pen. Then she went outside into the same darkness, the same rain.

Truth and Silence

'Everyone has the potential to be a murderer,' she said. And I laughed. She was wrapped up in that white fleece with the furry hood and her cheeks were flushed from the walk we'd just had along the coast. Waves were lashing themselves against the gritty shore. It was five months since she'd had the argument with her sister and two months before she disappeared.

There was never any sense of superstition. Just saying something wasn't going to make anything in particular happen. Not saying was often the best bet. There was a whole lot of stuff that got better all by itself if you just left it and Janey knew that. She wasn't one of those neurotics that keep poking things with a stick, again and again until the dead animal in the room began to smell. Dead animal. That's funny. I mean – strange, not funny, I hope you don't think ... well, anyhow. We never fought. Never fell out, not outright, not out in the open. Things just went cool, frosty. Of course now there are times when I wonder whether the way we were together was like a frozen lake, crusty but beautiful on the outside – but underneath there's all this shit, weeds and algae and shopping trolleys and half dead fish with the entrails trailing, murk basically. I didn't think that then. I didn't think anything. Inside my brain is like a room in the dark, empty except for a big worn armchair in the middle with no-body in it. I still don't think really unless someone comes up and says something to me that flicks some kind of switch. But no-one comes up anymore, they just do this backing away thing. If they see me coming along the street they slide themselves up against the wall and focus their eyes on a bright patch of sky or a signpost several metres away or their shoes or their phone cos people always have something incoming that just needs attention. They don't see me.

Anyway we were cool, she was cool, I was cool. And the flat was freezing. The bed was a small double but when she curled away at the edge with her long toes hanging out the side the cold air slid down the middle. No body heat when she made a space between us. But she used to bite my fingers when I put myself inside her and her sweat smelled of coffee.

Coffee on a Saturday morning when Saturday morning started post midday and the sun was already slanting by the time we'd had a wander down to the deli with the octopus ink spaghetti and the porcini in the long glass jars. When we got back she would put on some garlic bread and I would play the guitar quietly with my back to the wall looking out of the first floor window and the chords were strumming against the long shadows growing on the underneath of trees, and the high notes were picked out of the ochre glow on the leaf tops. Afternoons and sunsets. It was so quiet behind the music, behind the sizzling of onions in the galley kitchen. That wrapped round feeling, sun and sweet melancholy, soul in a bowl and the light fading.

'Everything is situational,' she said and the wind beat her hair senseless. Would we have ended up together if Mark and Ciaran hadn't stolen your taxi and it pelted rain and we both ended up staying at Angela's?'

'That's different, that's fate,' I told her. Knowing that was wrong as soon as I said it. 'No, I don't mean fate, like it's meant to be, I mean that was just something that happened. No-one made a choice.'

'You could have got wet. You could have sat on the sofa instead of on the floor beside me.'

'So how does that make me a murderer?' I asked but then this picture came into my head of us having sex and I'm on top of her and I'm holding the hair at the back of her head and then I'm putting my hands on her face and nothing is enough, the light is dim and I want more, I want to take her apart, I grasp her by the hair and pull and I push myself into her and I want to destroy her, I want to rip apart the silence.

Now she is laughing but it doesn't seem anything to do with me. It's not even a nice day weatherwise, there are all these low down grey clouds hanging guiltily around. The sun has slouched off. She picks up a stone, light blue with a line of white through the middle and she makes to lob it into the water but then she turns round and throws it at me. It hits me on the lip and I feel blood. 'What the ...' She is staring at me with a kind of frown, it looks like she's squeezed all her mind into the bit between her eyes but her mouth has shimmers of purple and blue and a smile is playing around it like light. 'I just wanted to get a reaction,' she said. Later we walked past a pub that served hot food and good beer on our way to the bus stop. We didn't go in. The warmth and the bubble froth of conversations would have interfered with the silence.

Later on the bus home she said 'There's nothing you can do to me because I don't love you.'

She believes in honesty. She uses honesty as a kind of currency. It buys her personal freedom. She can't help it if it's the truth. Can she.

That's what the argument was about with her sister. Truth. She wasn't going to pussyfoot around with the things she said to Certain Members of her Family.

Because she didn't get on with her mother and her Dad was long gone.

Her sister, Diane said that their Mum was concerned about Janey and couldn't Janey make an effort to ring her and patch things up. Janey said that her mother was the chewing gum on the soles of her family's shoes. Her sister said that Janey was cold hearted and paranoid and needed her head examining. Janey said 'instead of trying to sort me out, why don't you concentrate on sorting out your own brats.'

But Janey had moved into Diane's for two months to help out when Jade was still a baby and Dylan was three and Jade got really sick and had to stay in the hospital for tests. She told me this in between playing pool and the slots at the amusements one Sunday afternoon. The sun was blazing and busloads of people had turned up at the seafront. The Dads were wearing ice-cream and the babies were eating sun lotion and stick handed grannies were eating sticks of candy floss. The sun was too bright so we went inside and she beat me at pool two games to one. After she won the first game she came up to me and pinched me on the cheek and said 'You know you *are* kind of cute,' and she laughed so loud and bent over while she was laughing. She was wearing jeans and this skinny red top. She laughed out loud and her mouth was open wide and the same colour as her top. She was leaning on her cue. And the balls made a thundering racket coming out along the chute. She was dying to get started on the second game. I put them in the triangle. But she didn't win that time, she fouled a yellow and I took it from her and she went quiet. But in the last game she split the balls wide open and pocketed a red automatically. I didn't stand a chance. She turned my mistakes to her advantage, she found the chinks and stabbed me through them with the point of her cue. When she potted the black, she pursed up her mouth and she looked at me from under her eyelashes, her eyes dark pins, as if she thought I might take something from her.

We did the slots. She won four times on the trot. The pleasure of treasure clanging down the chute.

She never used to ask me questions about myself. I think she wanted to take things at face value. But she didn't really look me in the face either. In the early days we used to talk at the floor to each other and later she used to direct comments to long strands of her hair. And later again she used to look at the wall when I said something she didn't agree with and screw her toes into the rug. And at bedtime I got the long cool column of air up my back. I would fall asleep thinking what was her problem, what I'd said to her wasn't all that bad and anyway she never cried, never made a sound.

Sometimes when I came home from work and she was there before me with the telly on and her feet curled up and her thumb in her mouth and her twisting the guts out of her hair, I used to wonder why we were together. And were we together, or just taking slices out of each other as we slid past.

People say they never saw the end coming. That's because it's always there – like mercury in a glass ready to spill its poison. The end is always under the ribs, under the pillow, under the past sell-by-date carrots in the fridge, pulsing under the fingertips when you touch each others skin.

We had a raging argument one day. In fairness it probably wasn't about onions but I can't remember the details. She was spitting, sparking, roaring, wailing like a wild animal. God I so missed the cold shoulder, the silence. I thought I could see a glimpse of it like the eye in the centre of a tornado, this hard cold globe in the middle of me or of her. And I stayed still with her fury flailing around me like whips or thrown flame. I watched her crack wide open.

I didn't do anything. Believe me.

Janey used to say to me 'Whenever I say something I know the opposite could just as easily be true. When I say nothing it's because everything in my head cancels each other out. When you say nothing it's because there is nothing. Is there? Is there?'

Even when she is pleading her eyes are blank, dead.

Is it possible to kill someone just to make yourself feel something?

She just went away.

For ages afterwards I used to find long strands of her hair stretched over the furniture, in the shower, on my jacket, even once in my breakfast cereal, Janey DNA. I had to remove her from between my teeth and that was after she was, well, no longer here. For a while I couldn't get rid of her, toenail clippings in the bin, armpit shavings on her razor, the smudge of her fingerprints on the mirror. I thought that the police would take more notice, since they were trying to find her, but they couldn't seem to see what was in front of their face. They questioned me but then seemed to get bored. She had done this kind of thing before. Her mother even told them she had self-harmed at one point, drew parallel lines that oozed blood across her arm. 'I never knew what was going on in her head' she said to me when she came to the flat with Janey's sister, to take some of Janey's stuff. She hugged me when she came in. She smelled sweet and powdery, her arms were squidgy. She seemed real soft, the kind of sponge like person who soaks up everything. I said that I wished I could say more about what happened. I said that losing Janey left a kind of hole.

Now I remember Janey in her white fleecy hood and then with her little red top, looking at me, laughing. I guess I miss Janey. I should. I don't really think but sometimes I like to imagine her at the bottom of a frozen lake, making a racket. Kicking, shouting, blowing bubbles up to the underside of the hard ice.

Without The Light Pollution We Can See The Stars

Morrison was with Emily now. Mornings in the garden, stepping together from the far sides of a dazzling and billowing white sheet, losing each other among the wind--lifted fabric then finding each other again. These were ordinary, wonderful things in a new life that had been decided with hardly any words needed.

In the evenings – in this garden of the rundown cottage Emily had fled to – the thing that made Morrison happiest was the stars.

He did not know the names of stars like a poet should, he could not pick them out, even five or six from the billions. Narrowing it down to the brightest ones that were planets, Jupiter, Venus or Mars, he could make a stab at it with a one-in-three chance.

A one-in-three chance, of dying from cancer, like Emily's mother, of Emily finding the right man from a trio of candidates, her husband (ex), the rebel Eddie, and the poet – him.

Without the light pollution he could see the stars. In the night, blazed awake by mind meteors he went down, quietly, to the garden. On the right nights, so serendipitously that he felt a pain in his chest, shooting stars streaked hotly through the sky.

And he stood there breathless in the moment after. Shooting stars so random and chaotic so lovely and right, like the ideas and sensations that came at him from nowhere from which he would then write.

The stars are senseless he jotted down, with his notebook, blind in the country dark, hoping the writing would be legible in the daytime.

He had a dreadful memory, hence the notebooks and its recordings, sightings of Emily, fleeting wisps of phrases in the twilight, grasped like smoke and caught in a glass.

He could hear the trickle of the river and the great dark air was around him and the sigh let old emptiness out. Now his chest expanded again with the peace of the place and the reality of Emily lying upstairs in the cottage asleep and the girls who now called him Dad though he hadn't asked for it.

He sat, his feet amid moss and ferns, his bare toes cool in the grass.

He felt so young and endless here, out in the night, balanced at a moment that was right. He had not aimed for the stars, so he'd not fallen short. He'd worked in normal jobs, still had a Mum and Dad. He'd not had Emily's pain; losing her mother, extricating herself from a husband who fought with life. Though he found he could somehow understand her ex-husband, wary and blind to pleasure, to light.

The stars are senseless

He was always on the lookout for wonder, ever since he was young, always, long before he finally moved out here with Emily, Amy and Hannah. He'd always been beguiled by the romanticism of stars, their beautiful mystery, though they were so far away, or dead already. And yet the stars suggested some great white plain, beyond the dark. Some heavenly elsewhere.

Hinting, bright
At some great, blinding cloth
The opposite of night

Further back in time, there had been that day he saw Emily and her daughters on the long, unending beach of sparkling white sand. His future family.

White sands so soft and pulverised with time
And light, this aching light

Even though it took much longer until they were together, he recognised the moment on the beach as coming home, a kind of ballast, a landing. Now he sat on an immovable stone, the dark clear air all around. He saw a satellite traverse the sky.

Those tiny stars; hope stabbing through the dark

Since being with Emily he'd begun to look at people, not just fern heads and patterns in the sand. In the summer, back at his childhood estate, all the people gathered on the green chatting and children running about in swimming costumes with hoses and ice-cream. The sky was so hazy and bright, the sun was so strong and white hot. He had shielded his eyes with his hands and sunspots danced on the inside. Those beautiful faces around him, alive and delighted – the relief and flutter of conversation was like some exotic flower bud opening out.

Twinkle, the nursery rhyme said of the stars in the book of his new stepdaughter. He was not a parent but he could feel a new kind of love shine out of him for the child. He'd hugged the mother of the little boy on the estate who'd been run over and killed. Sometimes the black cloth of the sky was all you could see, nothing else.

But out here, outside of the city and its noise and threat on a clear night you could see the white of stars shining through as if from a bright expanse of white behind, like the sands on the beach on the day he'd seen his future family.

There was now a brightness in his life that he wasn't used to. Although nothing was forever.

The stars are senseless
Hinting, bright
At some great blinding cloth
The opposite of night
White sheets flung on a summer washing line
White sands soft, pulverised with time
And light, this aching light ...
Those tiny stars; hope stabbing through the dark

Morrison sat in the garden, the sky garlanded with those pinpricks of stars. He thought of how somewhere else the Earth shone for others, on this planet of random joy and tragedy. He thought of himself and Emily in daylight folding the sheets from the washing line together, walking towards each other at each fold, and then stepping away once more.

The Spaceman Has His Tea

The spaceman's cup clinks in the saucer. He looks at the liquid. The slight dash of milk has made it the colour of puddle mud. A stream of bubbles swirl into a central vortex, then pop and disappear underneath.

'Come round on Sunday,' his sister Claire had asked, 'It will do Hannah good to see you.'

He wasn't sure about that; though if he could do any good, he would, for Claire's sake.

'I'll invite Mother too. You can tell us all about the spaceflight. It must have been wonderful.'

He'd gone quiet at the other end of the phone line. The articulation of glory wasn't one of his strong points, nor was the expression of sympathetic grief. He simply didn't know what to say.

For a short time after he got back everyone wanted his story; daytime TV, popular science journals, the local papers, all looking for sound bites from space. He found himself within a great hubbub of rhetoric, voracious vernacular. The first time he saw the Earth, that bright globe in blackness, he'd expected the symphony of violins, the music of the sphere. But all there was only silence.

His white spacesuit crennellates at the knees where he fits them under the kitchen table. He lifts the teacup to his visor. Clink. Steams whorls in front of the glass. He places aside the cup, lifts the helmet, but fear makes him gulp. The air is thick with scent and hard to breathe. He puts back on the helmet. In space they imbibed through a straw, the action making them feel gloriously giddy like toddlers.

Claire had meant the tea for the garden, the weather had become so lovely. She had laid a white cloth on the patio table and started to transfer all the things out. She liked to be busy, she needed to be; she spoke continuously, lightly, like the high precarious notes of a violin. He said that if it was okay, he would like to sit out of the sun for a while. Sometimes he found it too bright out of doors ever since he'd returned to Earth, he told her.

She said that would be fine but she didn't linger in the kitchen once she'd poured him tea. She joined the others outside, leaving the plates of food behind, as if the effort of creating this celebration had, with those few words, become too much for her. Endurance, tenacity, these were the qualities that they had measured for before putting him on the space program. These were qualities he shared with Claire: she would keep going, despite what had happened to Hannah's dad – apart from these temporary glitches.

The spaceman appreciates his quiet reprieve. Since he came back the world has been yelling at him; articulated lorries on the ring road, trains screeching into sidings, corn fields, poppies, the beeps on his alarm in the morning, the thunderous hum of aeroplanes on flight paths to the hub, the smell of hot tarmac.

He holds the tea cup against his hand for comfort. The cup is hot, but he feels nothing under the gauntlets ringed with metal clips at the wrist.

Claire has gone to a lot of trouble, setting out the very best china, a set received as a wedding present. It is delicate, almost translucent, painted with a thin blue rim, reminding him of the fragile curve of the earth's atmosphere. He touches one of the empty cups with his fingers but the thick material makes him clumsy. The cup falls and chips. He picks it up in his slow motion hands, breathes against the inside of his visor, closes his eyes against disaster.

When the time came for him to make the trip, he'd worried about leaving them behind; mother had been on her own for several years, she had grown used to it, but Claire and Hannah's loss was still raw, disorienting. He'd felt strangely peeved by their upbeat farewells and good wishes, their lack of trepidation. But there was nothing to fear anymore. You could get killed just by clipping the central meridian on the motorway on your way home from work. You didn't need to go into space to be lost.

There is a small deck outside the sliding door with pots of begonias and geraniums and some steps down to a wide grassy lawn, edged with mature trees. In the far corner of the garden is an old swing, the seat slantways on worn rope. He can hear the modulation of female voices, the solace of their soft tones.

One of the voices is his mother's. She arrived a little earlier and greeted him with her usual delicacy and grace, for which he was grateful. She let him be and concentrated her attention on Hannah who held on to her grandmother's finger, dancing with impatience. She had something or other to show her in the garden, some treasure of absolute importance. Hannah had said 'hello' to him, her big eyes scanning his suit, her finger in her mouth, her body spinning forward and back on its axis.

Claire's shadow appears in the doorway. 'Is the tea alright'?' she says, approaching.

'It's a little strong,' he tells her.

'Have some of the cake,' she urges, 'we can have more later. I made it with Hannah – she insisted – she wanted to make things special.'

It is soft meringue, reminiscent of a vision of atolls and clouds as the space shuttle sped over the Pacific. On a nearby tray there are sandwiches piled up leaning against each other like the visible folds of continental plates collided. All the things they saw, a lifetime's worth. From space the Earth has sixteen sunsets and sunrises each day and every one of them is different.

'Come out and join us,' Claire asks. She puts her hand on his shoulder. 'We were looking forward to the company. Hannah is ever so excited. She said she was going through the questions she wants to ask you in her head last night.' Claire laughs, or seems to.

He sits still and wills her hand to lift. 'In a few minutes,' he says. Another sunset, sunrise.

The tea, the spaceman decides, is the taste of soil. When he was three he ate handfuls of black earth. Claire, two years older, used to scold him. At the same age he eyed the day's residual moon, he thought it was following him. Once he told his mother 'I flied up to the moon and held onto it.' He looked up into her face then, in his remembrance somehow golden. He was sure that she listened and believed him.

Outside it gets brighter, that feeling of bedclothes pulled back, that sudden revealing.

He eyes the trajectory of the worktop, its mottled pattern like the dendrites of ancient forgotten desert rivers still evident from above. He uses the counter like a guide rope, taking slow exaggerated steps across the kitchen floor.

He goes to the door and stops. He waits as he did for the airlock. He steps outside.

'If I stood on the moon would it feel more solid?' he wonders. Since he got back the Earth hasn't stopped spinning.

He discovers the heady scent at the bottom of steps. A rose planted near to the house. His mother's voice spills with relief on seeing him emerge. She tells him the name of the rose. 'This one is *Rhapsody in Blue*,' she says, all pleasure. He is envious of her white-haired naivety, her colloquial complacency. But she puts one hand on his face, outside of the helmet, takes his hand in the glove.

The shuttle arrived back into water; that held breath plunge under waves a rebirth.

When he was a small child choking with croup, she held his head over a pan of steaming water so that he could breathe. He departs from the roses, his mother's hand falls away like scaffolding from the shuttle as it launched.

Hannah is sitting on the swing, a girl in a sepia photograph. He notices the colour of her dress though, the hue of her eyes.

This planet is blue he thinks.

She swings competently now, higher and higher, without her father's hand that sped her into orbit as a toddler. She never felt fear, her face, all manic glee, her father laughing, her mother halted with smiling – a contagion of happiness.

There is a sliver of apologetic moon in the sky.

She launches herself from the swing mid-flight and lands with a thud on the yielding mud. He rushes over – like walking through water with this suit, now a hindrance. He bends down and reaches for her small body. 'Whoops,' she laughs.

He sets her back on her feet. Hannah dusts down her dress and looks at him.

'Were you really in space?' Did you land on the moon? Does the moon really have a face?'

'No I wasn't on the moon, but I drove past it. I went up in my rocket ship and looked down on the earth and all the things and people on it.'

Unleashed from the world is not to be free of it, it is to be put in charge of the last egg in the basket, it is to be six years old and have your mother put the egg into your hand and say 'Don't break that.' And the earth is as blue as a bird's egg, as precious as Fabergé, as fragile as Arctic ice.

It is to be six years old and afraid of forgetting.

Hannah looks at the moon. 'Sometimes I look out when it's dark and think about my Dad.'

A tear splashes against glass. The spaceman reaches up and takes off his helmet.

At nights he watches for satellites scudding across the night like rogue, adventuring stars.

'Space is very big,' he says. His voice in the air surprises him.

'I know,' Hannah taking his gloved hand. 'I might go there one day. I could get a spacesuit like yours.'

They go back across the lawn.

'When you looked down, could you see me? I was waving. I waved until my arm got too tired.'

He smiles down at her.

'Yes, I saw you and I waved back, but you were very small.'

Claire has finished laying the table, Hannah helps the spaceman out of his suit. They sit down, his mother to the left of him, Hannah to the right. He feels the sun's radiation from ninety three million miles away on his bare arms.

He picks up a sandwich from the plate, feels the springiness between his fingers 'Bread,' he says. He eats the bread.

Hannah stretches her hand out towards him.

'Look what I found.' It's a marble held between the finger and the thumb. A blue marble with a wave of lemon threaded through the centre. She puts it into his palm.

'You have it.'

He looks at the marble, the sun reflecting on it. Marbles never break. He puts it into his pocket.

Claire pours more tea. He picks up the cup. The warmth transfers to the tips of his fingers. He tastes the meringue, light, delicious; clouds dissolving on his tongue. And the world feels just right, like that just right planet on the other side of the universe that the scientists think might be ripe for life; a planet they could flee to, if this world falls apart. Claire sits down, conversation begins. And as he drinks the tea, perfect now, hot, sweet, reviving, he feels as if he has landed. As if he travelled all that way just to return for this.

Milton Keynes UK
Ingram Content Group UK Ltd.
UKHW051613300923
429576UK00015B/123